WHAT A TIGER WANTS

TIGER SHIFTERS 8

KAT SIMONS

T&D PUBLISHING

WHAT A TIGER WANTS

Copyright © 2017 by Katrina Tipton
All rights reserved.

Published 2017 by T&D Publishing
Cover art design © 2017 and 2019 The Killion Group
Interior book design © 2019 T&D Publishing
ISBN-13: 978-1-944600-19-8 (Trade Paperback Edition)

This is a work of fiction. All of the characters, places, organizations, and
events portrayed are either products of the author's imagination or are used
fictitiously. Any resemblance to actual persons, living or dead, business
establishments, events, or locales is entirely coincidental.

First printing: April 2019
For information, contact T&D Publishing www.TandDPublishing.com

Dmitry Chernikov parked his truck outside his older brother's cozy house in Eirene, Colorado, opened the driver's side door and pulled in a deep breath. Pine and snow, rich earth, squirrels, the faint scent of Nick's diner a short walk away on Main Street, and the definite scents of his brother, his sister-in-law, and—Dom smiled—their five-month-old baby girl.

He climbed out of the truck, stretching sore muscles and savoring the crisp, sharp bite of Colorado in December. The late afternoon sun hung low in the sky. He'd driven for several days to get here, stopping a few times to sleep but otherwise continuing straight through from West Virginia. He'd been spending so damned much time at the elders' US compound lately, helping his friend Victor Romanov with the compound's security, he'd barely seen the inside of his own home in Vermont. Not that it had much lure. It was just the building where he stored his stuff.

He looked in the direction of Nick's diner. Dom's heart had been in Eirene for a long time…

The door to Nick's house opened. Dom glanced back to see his older brother framed against a riot of bright, colorful Christmas decorations.

"Tiana says to come inside," Nick called, "before the ladies get a look at you and invade the house."

Dom rolled his eyes and snorted softly as he climbed the two wooden steps up to Nick's front porch. "That would be Mitch causing all the female rioting. How's Chrissy?"

"Sleeping so keep your voice down. I, on the other hand, haven't slept in months."

"You want a nap now?"

"Nah." Nick grinned. "Just need a little more quiet before the excitement starts again."

Dom had never seen his brother look so light and happy. Not since they were kids. In fact, Nick hadn't looked this easy and content since before they'd found their mother's body when they were both so young.

"What smells like peppermint?" he asked when the faint scent wafted out to him from somewhere close to his brother.

"Nothing," Nick said. "I don't know. Maybe Tiana's hot chocolate. Get inside before we freeze."

Dom raised his brows at Nick's weird tone but shrugged it off, figuring the sleep deprivation was getting to him. Dom stomped his boots off on the mat outside the front door—a new addition he attributed to Nick's wife— and walked into the house, shrugging out of the light jacket he used more as camouflage than for actual warmth.

"Who's cooking at the diner today?" he asked, then looked into the living room and spotted his sister-in-law. "Tiana. You look beautiful."

He spoke quietly because she was cradling a sleeping baby across her lap, one hand supporting the now quite large five-month-old and the other holding a tablet. The coffee table had been scooted close to the couch and held a cup of what smelled like mint-flavored hot chocolate.

Dom nodded to the cup. "Guess that is the mint smell."

Tiana looked past him to Nick with an amused expression Dom couldn't interpret. When he glanced at Nick, Nick was scowling.

"Hey, Dom," Tiana greeted, facing him again and smiling. "Come on in and get comfortable. Chrissy should be waking up soon. We weren't expecting you for a couple more days. I'm surprised Victor let you leave ahead of him."

The whole extended Chernikov clan was gathering in Eirene for the winter holidays and to celebrate little Chrissy's five-month birthday. Christina Loban-Chernikov was the first female born into the Chernikov family in more than a century—since Dom's grandmother, as far as he knew. Which meant Chrissy was going to be extremely spoiled and doted on. The five-month birthday celebration was actually his grandmother, the elder Elizaveta Chernikova's idea because she wanted another excuse to come visit her great-granddaughter.

"Last I saw," Dom said, "Alexis was dragging Victor

away from his ongoing campaign to keep the security at the compound from ever being compromised again. They'll fly into Denver at the end of the week."

"You drove?" Nick asked, motioning Dom into the living room. "Did they have a room for you at the motel or do you need to stay here?"

Dom took a free chair across from the couch so Tiana wouldn't have to turn too much to talk to him. The chair was large and soft, the light from a huge front window at his back giving the room a warm glow. There was a small fire in the fireplace, but a window somewhere in the back was open to keep the house from getting too warm for their higher tiger shifter metabolisms.

"I checked into the motel before coming here," Dom said. "And yeah, I drove from West Virginia. I needed the quiet."

Since he'd started helping Victor with the security at the compound—neglecting his own security business to do it—he'd been surrounded by other tigers almost constantly for months now. He never spent that much time with his own kind. Even his brothers, though they were close and talked a lot. He was, in a lot of ways, a stereotypical tiger—much happier on his own than surrounding by others.

Except, for some reason, here in Eirene he felt comfortable. Not crowded. Never hemmed in. Not even with the place full of other tigers—like it had been for Nick and Tiana's wedding back in May. Something about the place…

Or maybe it was because *she* lived here.

He shook off the thought, but it did remind him. "You

didn't answer my question earlier. Who's watching the diner?"

"That new cook who came into town a few months back. She's working out really well. Been doing a fine job giving me a little extra time to spend with Tiana and Chrissy."

"Which means you'll be buying her her own restaurant soon, then?" Dom asked, not entirely joking. His stoic, grumpy, occasionally broody big brother was a secret philanthropist who kept giving his best cooks money to open their own restaurants in other towns. One, a place in Vail, was starting to get international notice now. All because Nick fronted the owner enough money to open her restaurant.

Nick scowled. Tiana laughed softly. Chrissy snuffled a little in her sleep and rolled closer to Tiana, snuggling against her arm. Tiana smiled down at the baby's soft, fuzzy head.

"Anyway," Nick said, "Lulu has the grill, and Jane is minding the front."

Dom had perfected not reacting to the mention of Nick's head waitress over the last six years. He kept everything he was feeling neatly tucked under a casual screen of curiosity.

"How's Jane doing? Ben started college this fall, didn't he?"

"He did," Tiana answered. "Jane survived. But barely." She grinned. "She's better now, but I think that's because Ben is home for the winter break."

"Is he? I'll have to stop in and say hi."

"Bet he'd love that," Tiana said.

"I'm sure Jane will be glad to see you, too," Nick added without any hint of innuendo.

That didn't keep Dom from a knee-jerk suspicion that Nick already knew his secret.

Not that it mattered. Jane had made the situation clear when they'd first met, not long after Nick had moved to Eirene and Dom had come for a visit. She wasn't interested in dating or relationships. She was well and truly done with men. And the woman was just stubborn enough to mean it.

Dom decided thinking about Jane would get him into trouble, so he switched to other topics. "How are things with the wolf pack?" he asked Nick. "They're okay with another invasion of tigers at the edge of their territory?"

"Since the tigers are coming into my territory, it's none of their business," Nick said, his voice just a little deeper than it had been a moment earlier. "Their businesses in town are doing good—especially Siobhan Walsh's boutique."

"But?"

"But there's infighting." Nick shrugged. "You know how it is when a new alpha takes over. There can be years of settling out."

Dom nodded. He knew very little about wolf politics, and cared even less. But the Colorado pack's territory butted up against Nick's, close enough to be trouble. Anyone or anything that might cause trouble for either of his brothers was Dom's business.

"You hungry?" Nick asked. "I'm sure I can whip something up."

"You're tired." Dom waved him away. "For good reason. I'll go across to the diner, see how good this new cook of yours really is. Before you lose her." Dom stood and grinned unrepentantly at his brother's frown.

He crossed to Tiana and kissed her lightly on the head, letting his gaze linger on his new niece. A baby girl in the family. He was still a little stunned by the reality of it. None of the Chernikov brothers thought they'd have kids. He let his hand hover above Chrissy's soft, sweet-smelling head, afraid if he touched her he'd wake her up, then smiled at Tiana and headed back to the front door.

"You guys rest," he said, slipping into his coat. "While you can. I'll be back in a few hour."

"Say hi to Jane for us," Tiana said, casually.

"Will do." He turned toward the door but didn't miss the look Tiana exchanged with her husband. He just chose to ignore it.

Nick's diner was a classic, homey place, with tables lined in paper that children could draw on, wooden accents, and a Formica counter with bar stools facing the kitchen, visible through a large order window. It always smelled of delicious food and good, fresh coffee.

The entire town congregated at Nick's diner to eat and visit. This time of the afternoon, between the dinner and lunch rushes, the place was relatively quiet. Old Charlie Sanchez—an Eirene fixture—sat at the counter regaling a tourist with town "history," which if Charlie was telling it would be embellished past the point of recognizable fact.

Dom caught a few sentences and had to hide his smile—Charlie was telling a story about an ancient mythical beast that had stalked the area at night when Charlie was a kid, the beast preying on the unsuspecting.

If only Charlie knew the diner he sat in was owned by a "mythical beast."

A handful of other people sat at the tables and booths filling the dining area. Dom recognized a few locals, but the rest were tourists.

He sat at the counter, a few stools down from Charlie and his unwitting victim, and let the feel of the place settle into his bones. More than most anywhere Dom had ever been, the diner felt like home.

Though he tried not to make it obvious, Dom watched for Jane, carefully pulling in the various scents of the place, looking for hers… And there it was, under the perpetual coffee and grease smell, under the more pervasive, territorial scent of Nick and Tiana, the very faint touch of Jane's human, earthy, pine and fresh grass scent.

As if taking in her essence called her, Jane came out of the kitchen carrying a tray with two plates of sandwiches and fries. She was dressed in her work uniform—a pair of snug-fitting, low-rise jeans that always did amazing things to her ass, a light blue polyester shirt that should not have been sexy but somehow was because it hugged her glorious curves, and a short apron where she stored her pen and order book. Her thick, dark brown hair was pulled up into a bun, but tendrils of springy curls had escaped to frame her face, highlighting her high cheekbones. Her dark eyes were framed by thick lashes. Her full lips, as always, looked lush and kissable.

His heartbeat thudded hard and he flexed his hands against the counter, working to control the instant hit of lust.

She spotted him and nodded, smiling faintly as she carried the tray to a couple obviously in Colorado for the skiing.

"Be right with you, Dom," she said in passing.

He returned her nod of greeting and remained casually seated at the counter, not following her with his gaze, not straining to hear her speaking to the customers…and impressed he managed that much. He hadn't seen her since Nick and Tiana's big wedding bash in May, which wasn't unusual. He made an effort to go as long as he could without seeing her. Somehow he was always drawn back to Eirene, to Jane, and to the certain and hopeless knowledge that she refused to admit to the attraction between them.

He smiled in greeting when she rounded the counter, keeping the barrier between them, and stopped to pour him a coffee.

"How did you know?" he asked.

"Everyone needs coffee or tea at this time of the afternoon."

She looked up from the cup to grin, the expression crinkling the corners of her eyes in that way he adored. He wrapped his hands around the mug to keep from reaching for her.

"When did you arrive?" she asked.

"Half hour ago. Chrissy is napping so I thought I'd get some food. And try out this new cook Nick's hired."

"You're gonna be impressed. She's almost as good as Nick. What'll you have?"

You. Aloud, he said, "What's best?"

She narrowed her eyes at him, her mouth pursed as she considered. The expression drew his attention to her mouth and he almost groaned aloud. He loved her mouth. She had such perfect heart-shaped lips, and all he could think about in that moment was pulling her into his arms and kissing her hard.

"Think you'll love the fajita sandwich," she finally said.

He blinked and focused on her eyes. Which didn't actually help the erotic fantasies his imagination was torturing him with.

"It's one of Lulu's specialties," she added. "Be right back." She paused on her way into the kitchen, looking over her shoulder at him. "It's good seeing you again, Dom. Always nice to have you back in town."

He didn't let the pain show in his expression, but he was grateful Nick wasn't around because Dom's scent filled with a longing he knew was pointless. He should have stayed away, despite his grandmother's insistence that everyone be here. He really needed to keep as far from Jane as he could get. For his own mental well-being. She didn't want him, or any man for that matter—a small mercy—and she'd made it clear years ago that she wasn't ever going to change her mind.

The worst of it was, she was attracted to him. He caught delicious, tempting hints of it in her scent, and tormented himself by memorizing those elusive flavors of spice and want. If she hadn't revealed that much to him, if his *tiger* could just be convinced there was no hope, Dom was pretty sure he'd have been over this obsession by now.

His heart thumped harder when she came back out of the kitchen and he sighed quietly. Well, maybe not exactly over the obsession. But at least there wouldn't be even a hint of hope in his soul. There wouldn't be this nagging sense that maybe, just maybe she'd change her mind.

Jane forced a casual smile. She stopped at the counter again to exchange small talk with Nick's younger brother, and all the while she had a running monologue rolling through her mind, the irritating voice of her wiser self, telling her to get over this attraction to Dmitry Chernikov.

Stop acting like a silly girl. You're too old for this. You're too old for a crush on a man this young. He's not really interested in you so stop acting like a fool—even if only in your head.

She'd nearly dropped a hot pot of coffee the first time Dom had walked into the diner. Jane had stood like a lovestruck fool for what felt like an eternity, just staring at him. To this day, she wasn't sure what it was about him, exactly. He was sexy as all hell, and his eyes could turn most women to mush. But her boss was gorgeous enough to be a male model, and she'd never reacted to Nick that way. She'd been done with men for more than two years when she'd first met Dom, and she'd been completely unprepared for the impact he had on her, the way he'd turned her inside out.

A little taller than Nick by an inch or two, Dom was thickly muscled even though he was a computer geek—his words—which made her way too curious about what he did to earn those muscles. His hair was a little more brown than blond, and his hazel eyes sometimes looked green and other times more gold. His features were sharp and strong, his voice deep and husky. And his smile… His smile made her knees wobble.

When Nick had arrived in town, he'd turned the female population of Eirene on its head, but Jane had always seen him as…well her boss and a friend. She was protective of him, the way she was protective of the town. And she was amused by what other women had done to get his attention, but she'd never been attracted to Nick.

Dom, on the other hand… She'd felt like she'd been hit with a two-by-four when he'd smiled at her and had barely managed an intelligible hello when he'd taken her hand in greeting as Nick introduced them.

The last time Jane had reacted to a man that way had been…a long time ago and led to yet another very bad situation. Before Dom, she'd been certain she'd finally gotten over all the romantic longings nonsense she'd harbored in her youth. Dom proved just how wrong she'd been.

And she'd run from that attraction as fast as a woman could go. Not physically. Eirene was her home, and she'd be damned if she'd be chased away just because she got all hot and bothered by her boss' brother. The man didn't live here. She didn't have to see him all the time. But she'd rolled up all those girly feelings of desire and stomped them down deep, under her cynical, battered and scarred soul.

"How's the coffee?" she asked when she realized she'd been staring at him without speaking.

"Perfect. As always."

She needed casual things to discuss, stuff you'd talk to your boss' brother about. Nothing too personal. Nothing to hint that she was restlessly trying not to notice how good he smelled, or how fantastic he looked. His hair was a little shaggier than usual, a bit longer than the last time she'd seen him, and it was all she could do not to reach across the counter and brush a few stray strands off his forehead.

No! Act like the grown woman you are. Stop panting after the younger man. He'd probably be embarrassed for you if he knew what you were thinking.

"You staying with Nick?" she asked.

"No, I'm at the motel by the highway for the next few days. I didn't want to crowd them, with the baby and all."

"You'll get more sleep at the motel," she said.

Dom chuckled, and her thighs clenched. Jesus wept, the man had a sexy laugh.

"Elizaveta rented that cabin she loves," he said. "I'll move up there once the rest of the clan descends later in the week."

A beat of silence and she almost got lost in his eyes. Damn it. She blinked. "So how's your work going?"

"Good. Busy. Working with Alexis' husband at the moment."

At the mention of Nick's aunt, Jane smiled. She liked

Alexis. A lot. Woman was down to earth and didn't suffer fools lightly. Just the kind of person Jane could relate to. "She and Victor coming to the big family reunion Tiana's been gushing about for a month?"

His crooked grin sent an obscene amount of lust through Jane. She ignored it. Forcefully.

"They're coming," he said. "Bringing Isabella and Scott. James will be arriving a little late. He's got some college exams to finish or something."

"Good to hear. Good to hear." She bit the inside of her cheek to keep from saying anything else inane and shifted gears. "Ben's home for the winter break, too."

"Nick told me. How's he doing?"

"Seems to be doing well. What he tells his old mom, anyway."

"You must be proud of him."

"Too much for words," she said, with complete honesty.

"Think he'd like a visit?"

"He'd love it."

Her son adored Dom, and had since they'd first met and fell easily into talking about computers. Ben's conversation could be a little hard to follow sometimes—even now. At twelve, Ben had almost been able to hold a conversation like a neuro-typical kid, but he'd still stumbled over words and the order to put them in when he got excited about a topic. Dom hadn't even blinked, just followed Ben's rambling and disjointed discussion without missing a beat.

Jane had been attracted to Dom from the start, but she

was pretty sure she'd fallen in love with him in that moment.

Which had set off so many alarm bells in her head, she'd gotten a headache from them.

"How's Ben adjusting to college life so far from home?" Dom asked.

She blinked away the memories. "Better than my worst fears. The college has a group for kids like Ben, to help them adapt to the social stuff. He says he's enjoying it. It can be hard to tell with him, you know."

"How are you doing?" he asked with a knowing nod as he sipped his coffee.

She snorted. "As well as can be expected. Empty nesting and fussing like a mother hen whenever he calls. The usual. I'd have preferred him going to school some-where closer to home, but the local places didn't have strong support systems for autistic kids. And at least Wash-ington isn't a long flight from here."

Dom grinned. Her heart thumped faster. She ignored the reaction.

"He's at the house now," she said, "if you want to stop by after you eat."

She almost hated to invite Dom into her home—his scent lingered and tortured her—but she did every time he was in town. Ben was crazy about him, and Jane never had been able to refuse her son much when it came to socializ-ing. That was her excuse anyway. An excuse she acknowl-edged as bullshit only in the middle of the night when she couldn't avoid her own guilt.

"I will," Dom said. "Thanks."

A ding from the bell on the order counter drew her back to her job, a blessing of a distraction. She retrieved Dom's sandwich, then excused herself to fill coffee cups and check on the other customers, making an effort to chat and act normal. To her everlasting irritation and supreme embarrassment, old Charlie Sanchez flashed a gummy and lecherous grin at her when she filled his cup, waggling his eyebrows in Dom's direction.

Nosey old coot, she thought, scowling at him despite the heat crawling over her cheeks. Charlie just chortled wickedly and raised his mug to her in a silent toast. She glared a warning at him and stalked away, swearing she'd put him in his place as soon as Dom was out of earshot.

Then she'd put herself in her place, too. Because her lust-fueled obsession was too obvious if Charlie was teasing her about it. Her only hope was that Dom would continue to be a gentleman and ignore her inappropriate feelings. Someone had to be the grown-up.

Even if it was the younger man.

CHAPTER TWO

om devoured his sandwich, accepting as truth
everything Tiana had said about Nick's new cook
and making a mental note to eat at the diner a lot over the
next week before Nick helped Lulu buy her own restaurant,
or sent her to culinary school, or whatever other noble thing
he'd end up doing for the woman.

When Dom was finished and had paid, despite Jane's
insistence that his money was no good there, he wandered
back out onto Main Street, pulling in a deep breath as he
tried to clear Jane's scent out of his nostrils. Clouds were
rolling overhead, bringing with them a sharp, crisp taste of
approaching snow.

The ski resorts in the area were probably ecstatic. It had
been a good December for them.

He strolled down the street a ways, nodding to the occasional local he'd met before. The sidewalk trees were
strung with little white lights that would brighten the area

as soon as the sun set. Snowflake lights were strung over the main road, and most of the shop windows boasted some sort of seasonal decorations.

Tiger shifters didn't share the religious and secular holidays humans celebrated except as a form of camouflage. Whatever holidays were the most popular and prevalent in the countries they lived in, those were the holidays tiger shifters celebrated. Dom had always liked this time of year, and all the different holidays observed at once in the US, especially the focus on light and color. And food. He loved the focus on food.

He purposefully strolled past the werewolf-owned clothing boutique, just to get a feel for the place. He hadn't been so sure Nick made the right decision, letting so many wolves into his territory. But the boutique seemed to be doing a good trade, and he knew from Nick that they employed half a dozen Eirene citizens. Dom didn't really like werewolves and rarely interacted with them—or any other shifter for that matter—but if the shop worked for the people here, he couldn't argue with Nick's choice.

And he'd met the new pack beta, a good man named Adam Walsh. The fact that Dom liked Adam almost immediately did bode well for the health of the once gang-like pack. Jane had told him the stories about the way the pack had been tormenting Eirene before Nick arrived—though of course none of the humans in the town knew the pack were werewolves; they assumed they were human thugs. The very slight fear in her tone when she'd relayed the story of the previous alpha threatening an old man with a steel pipe had set Dom's tiger growling even though it was all in the past. Dom's tiger just saw the fear in the woman he wanted even if she hid that feeling well. Dom's tiger wanted to destroy anyone who caused her fear.

Fortunately for everyone involved, he had never had the "pleasure" of meeting the former pack alpha. Dom hadn't been even a little unhappy to hear he'd been overthrown—a process that meant he had to die. From everything Nick had told him, the new alpha was a much better leader. Which meant Jane was safer now. And that was all that mattered to Dom.

He hovered outside the boutique, half-pretending to study the little display of children's clothing in the window while he watched the comings and goings inside. Most of the customers seemed at ease, casually shopping, a few taking things off racks and heading to a set of curtain-covered changing rooms at the back.

But as he watched, Dom noted a more heated and tense-looking conversation near the counter. A woman with dark, reddish colored hair, her eyes narrowed, her mouth pursed, glared at a man at least a foot taller than her. He was smiling in a smarmy way as he said something Dom couldn't hear from outside the shop over the traffic. As the door opened and closed behind a customer, though, Dom caught the tone of the very quiet conversation. The man speaking sounded insistent and threatening.

Dom also caught the smells and was pretty sure the arguing woman and man were both wolves.

He was tempted to go in and investigate, but they'd know instantly who he was from his scent. They had to keep wolf business out of Eirene if they wanted to keep running businesses here—that was the deal Nick had made with their alpha—so they wouldn't want to say anything in front of Dom that could get back to Nick.

Instincts Dom couldn't explain hinted at trouble. All the Chernikov brothers had gotten good at spotting trouble over the years. Their "outcast" status among the tigers and the frequent fights of their youth had made them all hyper-sensitive to danger. Dom had always been able to *feel* a fight coming.

And what he was watching was a fight waiting to happen.

He hovered a moment longer, gathering what details he could when the door opened and closed again, then he moved on so the arguing wolves didn't take notice of him. He pulled his cellphone out of his coat pocket and texted Nick with his suspicions. They'd talk more when he went back to Nick's place, but he wanted to give his brother a heads-up. Just in case.

He'd reached the side street that would take him to Jane's house by the time Nick acknowledged the text. Stuffing his cell back into his pocket, Dom turned down the residential street with its cottage-like houses and almost non-existent front yards, breathing in the strong, pleasant scents of the pine trees that dotted the area and the burning wood from a few fireplaces. Clumps of grubby snow piled at the base of the trees, though a few of the yards still had thicker, cleaner patches of white. The approaching snow-storm would cover this area and add a sparkling freshness to an already charming stroll.

Jane's house was a ten-minute walk from Main Street, a

two-story bungalow that was small but well kept. A full porch fronted the house and was empty now as Jane had taken in the chairs and table she put out for the warmer months. She'd strung colored lights along the thick white wooden posts holding up the porch roof, and wound more lights around the rails alongside the front steps. The base of her house was stonework that needed a good wash, but the rock and shrub yard was tidy, and the house had been painted a soft moss color since the last time he'd visited.

He braced himself for the way Jane's smell permeated the entire home, then rang the bell, tucking his hands into the pockets of his jeans and scanning the surroundings as he waited.

Ben answered a few minute later, his dark hair messy, his blue eyes distant and distracted…until he spotted Dom.

"Hey, Dom!" He grabbed Dom's hand and shook before motioning him in.

Dom hid his grin at the boy's strength. He'd never been sure if Ben realized how strong he was for his age. And Ben had a tendency to misjudge physical contact. The boy was gentle in spirit but his handshake could pull a grown man off his feet. Dom had always been glad for his own shifter strength around him.

"How're you doing, kid?" he asked.

"I'm fine. How are you?"

"Good. Good." Ben glanced over his shoulder toward the living room and Dom frowned. "Did I interrupt something?"

"Working. Got a job. Did Mom tell you?"

"No. What are you doing?"

Ben motioned Dom to the living room—a cozy area with overstuffed furniture, a lot of books and magazine clutter, a large-screen TV across from the couch, and a screened-off fireplace snugged into the corner. On the coffee table in front of the couch was a paperback from Jane's favorite thriller writer sitting on top of a business management text book, a gaming console, and an empty glass Dom assumed belonged to Ben. Jane had set up a six-foot Christmas tree in the corner opposite the fireplace, near the front window, decorating it in all the colorful lights and ornaments Ben liked best—a detail Dom knew from previous year's Christmas trees. More swaths of decorative color covered the fireplace mantel, weaving around pictures of Ben and Jane.

The space wrapped around Dom like a blanket full of Jane's scent. He ignored his tiger's purr.

Ben sat on the couch and picked up the gaming console, clicked a button and started playing what looked to Dom like a quest-type video game. Though Dom made his living on computers, and liked the occasional puzzle game, he hadn't gotten into gaming much. He spent most of his time weaving down through layers of code, looking for cracks and vulnerabilities in a system's security.

He watched Ben maneuver through a world that looked bleak and dirty, trying to figure out the point of the game. Finally, he gave up and sat in a chair on the right side of the couch.

"Video games are your job?" he asked Ben, whose full attention was on the TV screen and the action playing out.

"Beta testing," Ben answered. "Developers send me their new stuff, and I see how long it takes to beat it."

"Do you always win?"

"Yes. The longer it takes, the better the game."

"How long did it take you to beat the best game so far?"

"Five hours." Ben looked up and grinned. "That was a good game." Then he focused on the screen again.

Dom laughed. Ben had a real eye for pattern and an ability to focus intensely on one subject—at least on the subjects Ben wanted to focus on—and that manifested in an uncanny ability to sort through puzzles and complex problem-solving games. A game that took five hours for Ben to finish would probably take an ordinary human several weeks of play.

"Good job, then," Dom said.

"Best."

"How's college?"

"Good."

"Any friends?" Dom asked.

"Yup."

Dom waited, then rolled his eyes and said, "Anyone in particular?"

Sometimes you had to drag information from Ben, especially when he was doing other things.

"Got a girlfriend."

That made Dom raise his brows. "Well done. What's her name?"

"Emma. She's autistic too but doesn't like labels."

"Fair enough. Did you meet her in a class?"

"Nope."

Dom waited another few moments, then said, "How did you meet her?"

"We're in the same group. They help us manage on campus."

"Is she pretty?" Dom asked.

"Yup," Ben said, and flashed another little grin at Dom before focusing on the screen again.

He watched Ben destroy the game he was testing and move on to a second one, which he'd just started when Dom heard a key in the front door lock. Braced for the sight of her, he was still overwhelmed when Jane walked in.

She hadn't changed out of her work clothes yet, which meant his fantasy of stripping her out of that polyester shirt roared to life, filling his imagination with thoughts of unbuttoning the shirt slowly, easing it open to reveal her skin inch by inch… Something about the way it pulled tight over her breasts sent his lust into overdrive every time—which was ridiculous because it wasn't exactly a sexy piece of clothing. But on Jane, it might as well have been lingerie.

The bun holding her dark hair up had loosened a little, with more tendrils of hair escaping to frame her face. Her skin was flushed from the cold, and her lips glistened slightly, as if she'd just licked them. Her scent hit him hard, that earthy essence that made him want to lick her every-where, to see if her skin was as delicious as she smelled. And it was all he could do to stay where he was, his hands fisted on the chair's armrests so he wouldn't reach for her.

He was so caught up in the sight of her, he forgot everything else around him. Just sat there staring at her like a teenager with his first crush.

She strolled into the room, slipped her scarf over her head, and dropped it behind Ben on the couch. She leaned over the back of the couch to kiss her son on the head, then frowned at the game he was playing.

"Which one is this?" she asked.

"*Squirrels of Battle*," he muttered.

"Looks stupid."

Ben snorted. "Is."

She grinned at his head then faced Dom, glancing around. "Did Ben get you a drink or anything?"

Dom finally stood, wincing at his bad manners—something his grandmother would box his ears for. "I'm good."

Jane rolled her eyes. "I'll go put on the kettle. Tea okay? It's too late in the day for coffee for me. I've got an early shift tomorrow."

"Only if you're making it. But really, I'm fine."

She waved off his protest and headed back out to the hallway, to the kitchen at the back of the house.

"When are you going to marry her?" Ben asked when she was gone.

The unexpected question startled Dom, and he turned back from staring at the spot where Jane had been to scowl at the kid. "What the hell are you talking about?"

"You need to get married." Ben didn't even glance away from the game. He snarled at something and cursed under his breath.

"Hey, language. Your mom is home," Dom scolded automatically.

"Sorry. Stupid game."

"What do you mean by telling me I have to get married?"

"You love my mom. She's lonely. You should marry her."

Dom's mouth hung open. He wouldn't have been more surprised if Ben told him to stand on his head and turn green. Dom had never even suspected Ben might notice the way he felt about Jane. It was more than a little disconcerting to realize he'd given himself away to a kid who didn't tend to notice social subtleties.

"Where do you get all this?" Dom asked, sounding gruffer than he meant.

"She likes you. You should kiss her."

Dom almost choked. "Ben, I think maybe you better leave your mother's social life alone. She might not like you telling me to kiss her."

"She wants you to. Why would she mind?"

"I..." Dom didn't know what to say to that. How the hell did he explain the complex and unspoken understanding between him and Jane to a young man who took everything literally and had to have figures of speech explained to him?

He was saved from figuring it out when Jane appeared with a steaming cup of tea.

She handed the mug to Dom, took one look at his face and frowned at Ben. "Alright, what have you two been talking about?"

"Nothing," Dom said in a rush. He narrowed his eyes at Ben, who shrugged and put on a new game.

Jane continued to glance between them, suspicion obvious in her expression and her scent.

Dom's heart pounded hard. He was still standing, too close to her now, and his imagination kept returning to Ben's words. *You should kiss her*.

He wanted to, almost more than he wanted to continue living. Every part of him reached toward that image of taking Jane in his arms, lowering his mouth to hers, watching her eyes drift closed as she welcomed him. The first soft touch of her lips against his.

He blinked in surprise when the tea cup in his hands broke apart. "Fuck," he muttered. "Sorry. Not sure how I did that."

Ben glanced at him, his brows raised. "Language. My mom's in the house." Then he picked up a tablet and started in on yet another game.

Dom opened his mouth, closed it and gave in with a helpless shrug. "Sorry," he said again to both of them.

Jane pressed her lips together in what looked suspiciously like a suppressed laugh even as she narrowed her eyes at the remains of the cup. "Don't worry about it. It was an old cup. Probably had a crack in it I didn't notice. I'll get some stuff to clean up the mess."

Dom flinched and glanced down at the wooden floor. Bits of the porcelain not still in his hands floated in a puddle of hot tea.

Jane returned with a small, plastic garbage can, some paper towels, a hand broom and a dust pan. "Did you cut yourself, get burned?" she asked, nodding to the clump of broken cup still in his grip.

"No," he answered automatically. Truthfully, he hadn't noticed one way or the other. His fingers could have been shredded and he wouldn't have known because he was too busy berating himself for letting his imagination get away from him. Again.

He dumped the remains of the cup into the garbage can and motioned for the paper towels. "Let me clean it up. I feel like an ass already for the damage and the mess. I'll only feel worse if you have to clean."

She grinned and handed him the towels. "Help yourself." She was still smiling when her gaze dropped to his hands and the smile was replaced by a scowl. "You did cut yourself." She grabbed his hand and hauled it close to her face.

The move pulled Dom so close he could feel her heat. The touch of her skin against his robbed him of any remaining sense. He just stood there, staring down at the top of her head as she studied his palm, every muscle in his body on alert and ready to take what his tiger wanted so badly.

She brushed her thumb over his wrist, and he sucked in a breath. Tremors of need flooded him and his skin tingled in their wake.

It took him much too long to remember that she would notice his healing speed soon. Those little cuts would be gone in a few more minutes, as if they'd never been…

He pulled his hand away gently but insistently. "It's nothing. I'm fine. Let me finish cleaning up."

"I will not have you bleeding on my floor because of

some damn fool male pride. Come into the bathroom so I can at least clean those out and bandage them."

The bandage would hide the fact that the cuts were healed, but going with Jane into a small room while she continued to hold his hand would be very very bad.

And yet he didn't argue with her as she dragged him out of the living room to the small first-floor bathroom just off the kitchen. He didn't resist when she held his hands under running water. He couldn't have moved even if he'd wanted to as she gently dried his skin and studied the no-longer-bleeding cuts.

Her slight, "Huh?" snapped him out of his desire-haze.

He tried, unsuccessfully, to pull his hand back. Jane's grip was surprisingly strong.

"These looked…worse in the living room." She glanced up at him, not quite meeting his gaze. "I just washed away blood, but I'm not seeing even a nick now."

"Must have looked worse than it was. I told you it was nothing." He swallowed hard, glad she wasn't a shifter who could smell his lie. He didn't like lying to her. But she didn't know about the shifter world, and he didn't want to endanger her by revealing it. What Jane didn't know, in this case, would keep her safe.

"I swear there was at least one serious slice, though. There was blood." She pulled his hand even closer, practically putting her face in his palm.

His pulse kicked up and every muscle in his body went tight in an effort to suppress what he really wanted to do. Her warm breath against his skin was a deliciously erotic torture because he could imagine that feeling all over his body.

Blinking hard, he tried one more time to pull his hand away. "It was just a little paper cut. Those can bleed and close up fast. The blood probably made it look worse." His voice had gone an octave deeper, and gravelly. Damn. He had to get out of this tight little room and fast.

His conscience and self-preservation instincts urged him to leave. His tiger urged him to step just a little closer.

Then Jane looked up, her direct gaze clashing with his. Ben's words echoed through Dom's head again: *You should kiss her.*

Yes, his tiger growled.

Six years of resistance evaporated like smoke, the pent-up longing rolling over him and taking control. He closed the last bit of space between them, lifted her chin with his finger, and touched his lips to hers. A soft, slow tease…just a taste, he promised himself. Just a little taste.

The scent of her desire rose up around him, spicing the air with musk and freshness, a scent like basil and dill, mixed in with everything that was Jane. Her lips opened on a sigh. And he stopped teasing and got very serious, very fast.

Wrapping his arms around her waist, he pulled her tight against him, groaning as her soft curves flattened against his harder body. He tasted her, savored her, a kiss that went deeper than anything he'd experienced before. Years of denial poured out in that kiss, years of want and resistance and desperation. He tightened his fingers in her work shirt and angled his head to take even more. Everything she'd give him, everything she'd denied for so long…

None of the lost time mattered then, because she was returning his kiss, her hands tight in his hair, her body flush to his. Her nearly inaudible moans drove him crazy, ratcheting up his desperation. Somewhere in the back of his mind, he was aware of her eighteen-year-old son in the house, that this kiss was all he was likely to get, maybe ever, but that only drove him to savor and take whatever she offered.

He couldn't have pulled away from her if the world were collapsing around him, so it was Jane who finally eased back. Her dark eyes were wide, her panting breath making her chest rise and fall quickly, her lips redder and just a little swollen. Her tongue flicked out to wet her bottom lip, drawing his gaze. He started to pull her in again, but she put a hand on his chest and pushed him back a step.

"No," she said. "That shouldn't have happened."

"It was going to happen eventually, and you know it."

"No. And never again. A kiss doesn't change anything."

"*That* kiss did. Don't pretend it hasn't, Jane."

"I said no. I mean no."

He shook his head. "Stubborn."

"Arrogant.

"Not arrogant, hopeful. For the first time in years, I'm hopeful."

"Don't be."

"You want me as much as I want you. You can't deny it now. And I'm tired of ignoring it."

"You're my boss' brother. You're too young for me. And I'm never letting a man into my life again. This is never happening, Dom. Please let it go."

"No," he said, echoing her stubborn refusal.

But his body was humming from their kiss and if he didn't leave now, he was likely to say something he'd regret, or push her too hard when she wasn't ready.

"I'll go. For now," he said. "But this isn't done, Jane. Not by a long shot."

He waved to Ben on the way out the door and stalked out into the cold. Snow was just starting to fall, coating the narrow sidewalk in slippery ice. He was halfway back to Main Street before he remembered he'd never cleaned up his broken tea cup.

CHAPTER THREE

Jane stood in the bathroom for a few minutes after Dom left, breathing deeply and trying to calm her raging heartbeat. Damn but the man could kiss. She had to brace her hands on the sink just to keep upright, her legs were trembling so much.

She hadn't let a man get that close to her in…oh years now. But she didn't pretend that was why she'd reacted so strongly. All it had taken was one little brush of his lips and she'd been ready to climb on top of him and ride him till morning.

She squeezed her eyes shut and cursed under her breath. Then she opened her eyes, blinked at the white tiled wall, and straightened her shoulders. She had to get dinner ready. She'd worry about Dom later.

After taking another moment to splash cold water on her face, she made her way back to the living room.

"Did he finally kiss you?" Ben asked without turning

away from the game he was playing on his tablet.

Which was probably good because heat flooded Jane's face and her mouth actually dropped open.

"What did you just say?" she asked very slowly.

"Did he kiss you? I told him he should."

"What? Why?"

"You want him to. Did he?"

She stared at the back of her son's head, trying to figure out what to say to that. She worked hard not to lie to Ben— at least not outright. Ben took things very literally, and she had to be careful with what she said and didn't say. But while she might not outright lie, she did keep things to herself. And she'd been positive she'd kept her feelings for Dom to herself.

She'd been very very wrong.

"What do you know about kissing?" she asked, stalling.

"I've kissed Emma."

"You did?" That was news. And a perfect distraction. "When did this happen?" It probably wasn't good for a mother to be so pleased to hear her son had kissed a girl, but with Ben, every show of typical, age-appropriate behavior made her happy. Him having a girlfriend he'd actually kissed was like a little bit of Christmas, though she was pretty sure most people wouldn't understand that point of view.

"She kissed me," he said. "When we were done with exams and going home for the break."

"Do you miss her?"

"Yeah." He didn't look up, but he dipped his head in a nod. "I like her."

"I'm very glad to hear it." She frowned a little. "Although, if you marry her, her name will be Emma Emmerson."

Ben looked over the back of the couch at her, his chin lowered and his beautiful blue eyes very serious with that "teenager" look she'd grown to both love and hate over the last few years.

"Mom, I'm not getting married yet," he said as if this was the most obvious thing in the world. "I'm only eighteen."

She pressed her lips together so she wouldn't laugh. "That's probably a good idea. Wouldn't want to rush things."

He nodded and turned back to his tablet and the app he was testing, though not before she caught his eye roll.

She grinned, but kept her chuckle silent. The smile fell away when she recalled she'd already been pregnant at eighteen, given birth to Ben when she was only nineteen. Looking at Ben now, that seemed just so damned young. She'd thought she was old enough to make the decision. She'd seen it as a way out from under controlling parents. She'd thought she was in love.

Just one of many bad decisions she'd made over the years.

With a sigh, she shook off the old guilt and said, "What do you want for dinner?" She glanced down at the remaining mess of mug and tea on her floor and squatted down to scoop shards of porcelain carefully into the plastic trashcan with the dust pan.

"You never answered my question," Ben said. "Did you

finally kiss Dom?"

"First of all, that's none of your business." She banged the dust pan a little harder against the can than was necessary to remove a sticking chunk of broken mug. "You should *not* have said anything to him. Secondly, he's too young for me—"

"He's two years older than you."

She sat back on her heals. "No, he's not. He's younger than Nick."

"Nick's older than you, too. He's forty-three."

"What? No." That wasn't possible. She'd been certain that gorgeous young man was…well, young. "How do you know how old he is?"

"I asked."

"What? Why?" She was saying that a lot this evening. She pushed her hair off her forehead before sopping up the tea with a wad of paper towels, careful of the tiny slivers of broken pottery still on the floor.

"I like to know people's ages." He waved a hand in the air. "It's a numbers thing. Nick is forty-three. Dom is thirty-nine. Their brother Mitch is thirty-four." He glanced back at her. "You are older than him." Back to his game. "Tiana is twenty-nine. Chrissy is five months old. Charlie is ninety-eight, but sometimes he tells me he's a hundred and seven." He frowned back at her. "I'm pretty sure he's lying when he says that."

"With Charlie, that's probably a safe bet."

Ben's frown deepened, then he nodded, as if he'd translated her sentence. "He exaggerates a lot."

"Yes, he does." She dumped the wet towels into the

trashcan. "Do you know how old everyone in town is?"

"Yes." He went back to his game. "Can we have chicken fingers and potatoes for dinner?"

"Sure." She was still reeling from the fact that her son had learned everyone's ages. Not that he had the ages memorized—that seemed exactly the kind of thing he'd do —but that he'd asked people…

"You never cease to amaze me, you know that?" she said to him.

"I know. Are you and Dom going to get married now that you know he's not too young for you?"

"No." She finished cleaning the floor, gathered the can, towels and dust pan, and stood. "I'll go make your chicken."

She hurried to the kitchen before Ben started asking about her and Dom kissing again, because if he did and he just happened to look at her, even Ben would notice her blush.

She put away the things she'd used to clean up the spill and turned on the oven to preheat. She should call Grace later, after Ben went to bed. She really needed to talk to a friend right now, and Grace had a history with men as disastrous as Jane's. She'd understand. Grace might even be able to talk some sense into Jane's fool head, which was full of impossible hopes.

The fact that Jane's view of both Nick and Dom had just been upended didn't help her balance at all. Things she'd assumed to be true had just been a story she'd told herself. An excuse. With Dom, she needed any excuse she could get, and him being too young for her was a great one.

Now the thin threads of her resistance were fraying. She wanted him something awful and that kiss had only made matters worse. She could taste him now, feel him, knew exactly in perfect, painfully sensual detail what his body felt like pressed against hers. She could recall all of that way too easily, and she had a feeling those recollection wouldn't go away any time soon.

Sonofabitch. How the hell was she gonna get out of this without yet another major disaster?

* * *

Dom sat on the porch in the dark, long after Tiana and Chrissy had fallen asleep, waiting for Nick to join him. Nick had gone to the diner that evening to sort through some paperwork and get things ready for the next morning. They hadn't had a chance to talk about the wolves yet, which was just as well. Dom didn't want to worry Tiana. She had bigger—or rather smaller—things to worry about.

But this was Nick's territory. If there was trouble brewing, Dom wanted to help.

Besides, it kept his mind off Jane. And that kiss. The utter perfection of a kiss that was going to keep him restless and edgy for days. There was no going back now. No pretending to just chat casually with her, ignoring the desire they both felt. No way to go on without kissing her again.

He just didn't know how to get past her resistance.

He leaned back in the all-weather wooden seat and braced his booted feet up on the railing around the porch, letting the cold seep into his bones, taking in the scents and sounds of the night, pine and freshly fallen snow, the distant screech of an owl, the occasional car rolling down Main Street. The night sky had a faint glow, cloud cover reflecting light back from the snow, giving the darkness its own kind of soft lighting. Dom loved the way the night looked here, especially on nights like this. It reminded him of the good days when he was a kid, living in Montana, when his mother was happy and the haunted look in his father's eyes wasn't so obvious. When it had been Nick and him running free over the open country, stalking through the trees and pretending to be explorers.

As he heard Nick approaching on foot, he wondered if his big brother ever thought of those days, the good days before their mother's suicide and their father's mental break. Nick had had to grow up fast after that, taking care of Dom and baby Mitch. It was only now, as a grown man looking back, that Dom recognized how hard that must have been on Nick who'd only been nine years old at the time. Dom had always been grateful Mitch had been a baby, too young to remember those first few years of turmoil.

He shook off the moodiness and nodded in greeting as Nick took the steps to the porch silently, settling into another chair next to Dom.

"Been waiting long?" Nick asked.

"A bit. I wanted to give Tiana and Chrissy plenty of quiet to sleep. While they can."

Nick snorted. "Everyone keeps promising me Chrissy will start sleeping through the night soon. I'm starting to doubt it."

Dom chuckled. "How's the diner?"

"Still in the black. How was your visit with Jane and Ben?"

"Ben's good."

"And Jane?"

"Not going to talk about it."

Nick kept his gaze on the trees surrounding the front of his house as he said, "Something finally happen between you and Jane, huh?"

"Not talking about it."

Nick nodded. "She's stubborn. You've got your hands full there."

"So the wolves…" Dom did not want to discuss his feelings for Nick's head waitress. "I'm assuming the female wolf was the owner of the boutique, Walsh's sister?"

"Siobhan, yeah, she's there most days so it's a good bet. She's a smart business woman."

"Shop looks like it's doing well. Any idea what the argument was about?"

"I sent a message to Adam, checking in. His alpha has his hands full."

"Gonna cause you trouble?"

"Not if they want to keep their sister's store open in my territory."

"What's happening?" Dom had a feeling Nick was keeping a lot of the wolf conflict to himself so Tiana wouldn't worry. He couldn't blame his brother for that, not when Tiana was looking after such a precious new life.

Nick glanced back at the house, silent for a few moments. Finally, he faced Dom. "The usual infighting seems to have gotten a little nasty over the last month or so, according to Adam. Even though he fully supports his brother as alpha, it seems some of the pack are trying to pit Adam against Gabriel, pushing for Adam to take over."

"Why?"

"Adam won't explain it, but I get the feeling it has to do with some of the wolves who didn't mind that last, incompetent alpha they had."

"The one you fought with?"

"Yeah. He encouraged a lot more violence. He was a thug and the wolves who liked that kind of vicious rush don't like the rules Gabriel is setting down now."

"They think the beta will be any different? I got the impression he wanted stability as much as his brother."

"He does. But if he's forced into a fight with his brother for alpha position, it'll have to be a fight to the death."

"Are the brothers close?" Dom held Nick's gaze, thinking of their relationship, the tight bond he had with both of his brothers. He'd kill for them, and die for them, without giving it much thought. He couldn't imagine being forced into a death fight *with* one of them.

"They're close," Nick confirmed.

"How could they be forced into a fight then? Can't the beta just refuse?"

Nick shrugged. "Don't know entirely. Again, Adam won't get into that much detail about the inner workings of the pack."

"Can't blame him for that," Dom commented.

"Yeah. But the infighting spilling into Eirene is a deal-breaker for me. I made that clear tonight. So we'll see what happens."

"You need help, let me know."

Nick smiled. "Thanks." He patted Dom on the shoulder, then faced the surrounding forest again. "You sure you don't want to talk about Jane."

"Positive."

"I like her. She's a good woman."

"She is."

"Elizaveta would approve."

"I am not looking for our grandmother's approval."

But a part of him was pleased to hear that. Elizaveta could be a pain in the ass, which was sort of her job as an elder, but she'd always been an excellent grandmother. The fact that Dom had fallen for a human—not a hybrid who could give him kids like Mitch's fiancée, or a full tiger female like Nick's wife, but a human woman who he'd never have biological kids with… Well, most male tigers had to face that kind of a future. There were just too damned few tiger females. Dom had still worried, though, that Elizaveta would think he'd settled for a human. If she thought he was settling, she'd be difficult about it all and make things tough for Jane. That was, if Jane ever decided to give Dom a real chance…

At the idea of Jane facing off against Elizaveta, though, Dom smiled. Jane would be well able to stand up to his grandmother.

"I'll repeat, you've got your work cut out for you with Jane," Nick said into the extended silence. "She's got baggage she won't let go of easily."

"Everyone's got baggage," Dom said.

Nick snorted in agreement.

"Don't worry about me and Jane. It'll happen or it won't."

"It's the 'won't' I'm worried about. Tired of seeing you mope around like a lovesick teenager."

"Look who's talking, Mr. I'm-too-much-like-Dad-to-have-a-mate. Tiana shot that argument all to hell, didn't she?"

"Don't start or I will kick your ass for the fun of it."

"You wish."

"You want a beer?"

"Sure. When are Mitch and Nila arriving?"

"Day after tomorrow."

"It'll be good having everyone in one place again."

"Certainly will." Nick rose. "Be right back with that beer."

Dom smiled as the door clicked closed quietly behind Nick. He'd missed his brothers.

"Jane!" Grace answered the phone immediately, her voice bright and happy.

Jane smiled despite her glum mood. She leaned back into her couch, speaking quietly because Ben had only gone up to bed a few minutes ago. "I kissed him."

"Your boss' hot, sexy younger brother?"

"That's the one. Although it turns out he's older than I am."

"Really? So that means that sexy hunk Nick is older than you, too?"

"He is. Ben knew all along."

Grace chuckled. "Well there goes the 'too young for me' excuse."

"Yeah." Jane groaned.

"Good kiss?"

"Unfortunately."

"Guess now you're done-for."

"That's not what I wanted to hear."

"Sweetie."

There was so much sympathy in that single word, Jane almost teared up. "I'm not sure what to do."

"I know I haven't meet this man, but I like his brother a lot. Your boss is a good man. Isn't it just a tiny bit possible Dom is a good man, too?"

God, she wanted to believe that. Too much. And that was the problem. "You're one to talk. You and your sister couldn't be any different if you tried."

"I'm hardly the best example. And just because I have a bitchy, judgmental relative, doesn't mean all siblings turn out to be opposites. You've even said Dom is a lot like your boss."

"Except I'm not attracted to Nick. The fact that I'm attracted to Dom means there's a flaw in him somewhere, and I'm going to get hurt."

"You don't know that. You're not destined to keep repeating past mistakes. That's fear talking."

"You sound like your therapist."

Grace laughed. "I've been seeing her so long, I probably should have a psychology degree by now. You're still letting fear get the best of you."

"Damn straight. I can't help it, Grace. I've never once made a good choice in men. Not one single damned time in my whole life."

"But you've grown a lot in the last eight years. You're stronger than you were when we first met. You're not looking for someone to rescue you anymore."

"I was never…" But she cut herself off as Grace's words sank in. Ben's father had filled that role in a way, *rescuing* her from a stifling family life. But the others… She sighed. "Okay, say you're right about me looking for someone to save me. What makes you think anything is different?"

"Jane, you've saved yourself." Grace spoke as if that should be obvious. "All these years, you've looked after yourself and Ben, made a good life for both of you, all without any man to take care of you. You're the one who rescues people now."

Grace didn't say it out loud, but it hovered in the pointed silence between them, the reminder of the last time Grace had come to Eirene for a visit. Jane had had to tell Grace her newest boyfriend was hitting on every woman in town while Grace wasn't looking. After Grace had kicked the asshole to the road, she'd stayed with Jane, and Jane had looked after her for a week, helping her get over yet another disaster with a man. Jane had simply seen that as payback for all the good things Grace had done for her. They both had terrible taste in men. Jane saw it as her role as best friend to help Grace through the mistakes. She was protective of the people she loved, that was all.

She shook off the thought. "I'm just who I am."

"But who you are is enough. More than enough. You're a lot stronger now, Jane. You need to consider the possibility that this time you aren't making a mistake."

"I can't," she said, her voice strained and quiet. "I can't risk it. Not again."

"What are you going to do, then?"

"I'll have to tell him no more and be done with it."

"Can you do that?"

"I have to."

"Well, no matter what you do, you have my support. You know that."

"Thank you."

"You know, I was going to hide from my sister and her family in Austria for Christmas but I could change my plans. You want me to come to Eirene? I could check out this man, give you my unbiased opinion? Back you up?"

Jane smiled. With Grace's support, she'd definitely be able to resist Dom. "When can you get here?"

"I'll be there by the end of the week."

They settled their plans and Jane hung up, feeling a little better than she had hours earlier. If she could just put that wall back up between her and Dom, she was sure everything would be okay. Grace would help her. This wouldn't turn into another disaster.

But she went to sleep reliving Dom's kiss, and the part of her she couldn't trust kept reminding her how much she wanted to repeat that experience.

CHAPTER FOUR

Jane knew she couldn't avoid Dom for long, not without calling in sick, and she never did that. It was a point of pride. Plus, she rarely got sick, so Nick would know something was up. But she went into work that morning all on edge, both wanting to see Dom and dreading the moment he walked into the diner.

She always felt that way when he was in town, but now, after kissing him, that feeling was an awful lot worse.

With a great deal of effort, she kept her focus on the breakfast rush, serving the customers and passing pleasantries with townspeople as usual, keeping Nick—who was on the grill—on his toes, confirming details for a book club meeting with her friend Rachel when she stopped by for breakfast, keeping herself too busy to watch the front door. The effort worked for the first hour or so, when things were hopping and she had too much to do to pause and think.

During a lull in the pace, though, she started watching

the front door. Then cursed herself for her weakness and tried to find something else to think about… Her gaze landed on her son, sitting at the counter and talking to Charlie Sanchez.

Ben had walked her to work that morning—a show of maturity and chivalry that made her grin. He'd stopped asking if she'd kissed Dom and switched to telling her about the app he was helping to develop, which was a relief. Now, Ben chatted animatedly about some game with a bemused looking Charlie, Ben oblivious to the fact that Charlie had no idea what he was talking about. It didn't matter. Charlie gave Ben his full attention and nodded at all the appropriate places.

Jane's heart squeezed tight at the sight. That, the way the people of Eirene treated Ben, that was the reason she loved this town. That was the reason she'd do whatever it took to protect it. Because they loved Ben almost as much as she did, and no one had ever made him feel like he didn't belong.

She'd always liked to compare Eirene to the Island of Misfit Toys, all of the residents damaged in some way, but here, together, they were accepted and whole.

Jane ambled up to Ben and Charlie, catching a little of the story Ben was telling. "You two need anything else?"

"Orange juice," Ben said. "Thanks."

"How about you, Charlie? Want some more coffee?"

"You bet, Jane. And add a little something special to that if you've got it." Charlie winked, his dark eyes twinkling through the heavy wrinkles.

"It's too damned early for booze, Charlie." She leaned

in close and whispered, "But I'll see what I can find." She winked back.

Charlie cackled and patted her hand before she walked away.

She was returning to the counter with the hot pot of coffee when the little bell over the door jingled and Dom came strolling in, all six and a half feet of gorgeous male. Jane froze in place for a second too long, a moment's lapse that was way too obvious, like a deer in headlights. Dom's gaze zeroed in on her as if he'd been expecting her to be in exactly the spot she was in. He didn't even have to hunt the still-crowded diner, just looked right at her the moment he walked through the door. His expression was serious, intent, and entirely too sexy for words. Jane felt that look hit her square in her lady parts, and it was all she could do not to melt.

Damn the man.

She nodded in greeting, but didn't smile as she poured Charlie's coffee.

Ben and Charlie were looking between her and Dom, Ben's expression neutral, Charlie's full of knowing smugness.

She ignored that too and said to Ben, "I'll be right back with your juice."

Feeling like a coward, she escaped into the kitchen, careful not to look at Dom again. Her knees were actually wobbly from the adrenaline of lust and anxiety, and she had to lean against the work table for a moment to keep upright.

"Dom here?" Nick asked without looking up from the grill.

"How the hell did you know that?"

He grinned at her over his shoulder. "Eyes in the back of my head, Jane."

She snorted. "Right. Yeah, he's here. Better put on a bigger pile of bacon."

"On it. How're things going out there?"

"Busy. Good. Ben's telling Charlie stories."

"That's a reverse of the usual flow of information. How's Charlie taking it?"

She laughed outright at that. "With good grace. Table ten still needs that toast." She got Ben's juice, braced her knees, straightened her shoulders, and headed back into the dining room, determined to act normally.

That determination lasted a full second, and then she spotted Dom sitting on the other side of Ben, looking all hot and kissable and too damned delicious for this early in the morning. The fact that she couldn't seem to control herself around him left her grumpy, which was her excuse for her greeting.

"You eating or just taking up space?" she asked Dom.

From the corner of her eye, she saw Charlie raise his eyebrows at her, and she turned her glare on him. He lifted his hands in surrender, then picked up his coffee, still smirking at her.

"Bacon and eggs," Dom said, ignoring her rudeness.

Which only made her more irritated. "Be right back." She set Ben's juice in front of him, but he was too busy drawing something on a napkin to notice. She waved her finger under his nose and he looked up. "Don't forget your juice," she told him. Then she went back to place Dom's order.

She was such an idiot. She had to get better control of herself. Taking her foul mood out on Dom just because he was making her feel things she didn't want to feel was childish.

The bell over the door dinged again and Jane glanced over irritably, but her annoyance evaporated instantly when she spotted Mindy Jenkins, the owner of the antique shop. Mindy looked frantic as she rushed up to Jane.

"Is Nick here?" she asked. "There's trouble brewing outside the new boutique."

"Where's the sheriff?"

Mindy puffed out a frustrated breath. "He and the deputies got called out to the motel this morning, some bachelor party turned into property damage or something."

"Damn. Nick," Jane called into the kitchen.

Nick stalked out of the kitchen, his expression hard and dangerous.

"Looks like trouble outside the boutique and the sheriff's not around," she told him.

He glanced at Dom and without a word, both brothers hurried out of the diner, crossing against traffic to the boutique two doors down from Mindy's antique shop.

Jane hovered in the diner door, watching Dom and Nick approach two men standing over the boutique owner. The woman was glaring up at them, but both men were twice her size and standing way too close. Jane didn't have to hear what was being said to recognize an argument and a looming fight.

She forced herself to stay where she was, but anxiety clawed at her as she watched the scene unfold. She recognized one of the men. He'd been part of the group that had tormented Eirene before Nick had arrived and drove them out of town.

Mindy stood next to Jane, twisting her hands together. "Couldn't hear what they were saying," she told Jane, "but the tone sounded bad."

"You recognize that one guy?" Jane nodded.

"Sure do," Mindy said. "If this starts up again, I'm thinking I might ask Joe Sanchez for a few more…" She glanced at the crowd behind them and in the diner windows watching the brewing argument, both locals and tourists. "More of those things he makes," she finished, because of the tourists.

Jane was thinking the same thing. She patted Mindy's hand. "Nick and Dom'll take care of it." She forced herself to believe that.

One of the two thugs turned to face Nick and Dom, the other continued to glare down at the shop owner who was returning that glare in equal measure. Words were exchanged, though Jane couldn't hear what they said.

Only the fact that there was no one else to watch the diner and Ben was inside kept Jane from trotting across the street to help. Her heart was thumping hard with an old, primitive fear that sent a kind of panic into her blood, a feeling she resented to this day, and the part of her that had grown stronger over the years wanted to fight that panic by stepping into the middle of the argument.

The thug Jane recognized got into Nick's face. He was not quite as tall as Nick but close to being the same width.

Dom put a hand on the man's chest and pushed him back a foot, Dom's serious expression never changing.

The man made a lunge toward Dom. Every person in the diner watching drew in an audible gasp. Dom braced himself. The other thug grabbed the first by his arm, preventing a full-on attack. More words were exchanged. And then a car slid up to the sidewalk just behind the brothers, parking illegally. The Chernikovs didn't even turn to look at it, but the two thugs narrowed their eyes at the car.

From her place, Jane couldn't see the driver until he stepped out. Then recognition came immediately, the family resemblance between Dom and his brothers strong. Mitch Chernikov strolled up to the tense scene, patted his oldest brother on the back and said something, his expression pleasant and charming.

Beside Jane, Mindy sighed long and loud.

"What's all that sighing about?" Jane asked her without looking away from the brewing fight.

"Those Chernikov boys are just so damned handsome," Mindy said. "Seeing them all together never gets old. Shame they're all taken."

"Mindy Jenkins, you are a married woman." Jane scowled. "Besides, Dom's still single."

Mindy raised her brows at Jane, her mouth lifting in a slight smile. "Is he?"

"What the hell are you implying?"

"Not a thing, Jane." Mindy looked back at the standoff, still smiling, her expression blatantly, unconvincingly innocent. "Not a thing."

Jane glared at the side of Mindy's face, then turned

back to Dom and the others, ignoring the heat warming her cheeks. "Nosey woman," she grunted.

Mindy chuckled softly.

Dom kept his attention on the two male wolves as Nick ordered them out of town. He recognized one of them as the man who'd been arguing with Siobhan Walsh yesterday. The other was a stranger, but his musky, wet-dog smell made Dom's nose twitch. He very rarely interacted with werewolves, but about half of the ones he'd met over the years made his nose twitch.

"This is none of your business, kitty cat," the thug from yesterday's argument in the boutique said to Nick.

"Is in my town," Nick said. "My territory. My rules."

"Only because Gabriel is a pussy. This is our territory. You're squatting."

"Paid good money for this land. To that weak-ass bastard you called an alpha."

The wolf got into Nick's face. Nick didn't even blink.

"You think you're so tough, kitty?" the thug asked.

Before Nick answered, Dom put his hand on the thug's chest and pushed him back a foot, keeping him well clear of Nick.

"You want to try me, asshole?" the thug said.

"Don't need to," Dom said. He gave the wolf a once-over. "Wouldn't be much of a fight for me. Too easy. Where's the fun in that?"

The thug lunged at him, Dom braced for the attack, but

the other male wolf grabbed his arm before he could finish the attack.

"We're not here for this, Frank," the second wolf said.

Frank growled at Dom. "You and I aren't done yet."

Dom raised his brows. "You're even stupider than you look."

Siobhan snorted a half-laugh at that, earning a glare from Frank.

And then a car rolled up to the curb behind them. Dom didn't need to turn to see who it was. He'd felt Mitch approaching. Which officially tipped the numbers in their favor. While all three of them could easily take the two wolves on their own, the fight would get messy, and they had an audience of humans just across the street.

Jane was just across the street…

He pushed the thought away. She was safe. So long as they got the damned wolves out of town.

Mitch clapped Nick on the shoulder. "You fellas need any help?"

"Got it under control," Dom said, his gaze on Frank. "Not much of anything worth worrying about here."

Frank growled, a deep resonant sound that showed his wolf a little too close to the surface. Dom held his gaze, unblinking. Frank's gaze shifted to Dom's ear, a loss of dominance that made Frank curse. He continued to glare at Dom without actually meeting his gaze directly for more than a few seconds.

"Time to leave," Nick said, his voice low. "My territory, my rules. You break those rules again, there'll be consequences."

"The little bitch can come and go? We can come and go," Frank growled.

"Come on, Frank," the other wolf said, keeping his gaze on Nick even as he pulled Frank back from the fight. "We've said what we came here to say." He glanced down at Siobhan. "You need to take what we've said seriously. The time is coming for change."

She sneered at them, her only reply.

Frank snarled at Dom as he was pulled away. "We'll settle this soon." Though he still couldn't meet Dom's gaze for more than a flickering second.

Dom raised his brows, his only response.

The two males climbed onto a couple of motorcycles parked in front of the boutique and thundered off, leaving an echo of noise in their wake.

Siobhan watched them go, then faced Nick again.

"I'll be wanting to speak with your brothers," Nick told her. "Tonight."

"This wasn't their fault," she said, her shoulders straightening defensively.

"But as alpha and beta of the pack, it's their responsibility."

Siobhan's shoulders slumped just a little. "You gonna make me close the shop?"

Nick stared at her for a long moment before saying, "Not yet." He nodded back to her open front door. "Better get back inside. Expect questions. We have an audience." He didn't even motion toward the diner, but her gaze flicked across the street to the humans hovering in the diner windows and spilling out onto the sidewalk in front.

"I'll take care of the questions," she said. Then, somewhat hesitantly she added, "Thanks."

Dom couldn't decide from her tone if that was a grudging thanks or a grateful one, but her musky wolf scent carried a little of both as she returned to her store.

"Well, that was a fun way to arrive," Mitch said, grinning at them both. "Lucky I came along to protect you two."

"Right," Dom said.

Mitch chuckled. "So what's all the excitement about?"

"Wolf politics," Nick said, his gaze straying to the diner. "Tell you later, when we don't have civilians around."

"Right. What's to eat around here?"

"Got omelets and bacon going," Nick said. "What are you doing here already?"

They started back across the street, Dom falling in behind his brothers.

"That lion at the Bronx zoo is still having some trouble, so Nila sent me ahead. She'll be here as soon as she can." He paused and sniffed at Nick. "What smells like peppermint?"

"Nothing," Nick said, his tone more defensive than when he'd faced the wolves. "You want food or not."

"Food," Mitch said. "Always food."

Dom listened to the exchange with only half his attention. The rest was on Jane, still standing in the diner doorway, her lips pressed tight together, her grip on the door jamb turning her knuckles white. She blinked and met his gaze, the worry still clearly there despite the fact that the wolves had left. Her being worried about anything made his tiger growl.

"Everything okay now?" she asked Nick as they reached the door.

"No problem. All taken care of."

Mitch greeted Jane with a kiss on the cheek. Dom noticed with no small annoyance that she accepted the gesture without comment. She motioned Nick and Mitch past her into the restaurant, her gaze again locked with Dom's.

"That gonna be a problem?" she asked him quietly. "One of those guys, the one that got in Nick's face, he's been here before, part of the gang that harassed us until Nick took care of them."

Dom bit down his tiger's instinctive growl. "We'll take care of it, Jane. You don't need to worry."

"Those thugs come back, it'll be bad for the town."

He touched his fingers to her cheek before he could stop himself, dropping his hand in the next instant so she didn't have time to pull away. "Don't worry. We'll make sure you're all safe."

Her shoulders relaxed just a little, some of the tension easing in her expression. "Thanks," she said with a faint smile.

Next to her, the owner of the antique shop, a woman named Mindy Jenkins, hummed under her breath. Jane glared at her. Mindy smiled at the glare, managing to look both innocent and guilty all at the same time.

Dom frowned at both women, his eyebrows raised in

question. Jane rolled her eyes and stalked back inside the diner.

Mindy grinned up at him. "Good to have you back in town, Dom."

She followed Jane into the diner, leaving Dom more than a little confused.

CHAPTER FIVE

Dom stood across the street from Jane's house, listening to the night sounds, debating going up to her door. Last night's snow had left the neighborhood covered with a fresh layer of white, making the plowed street look black in contrast. Overhead, the sky was clear and star-dotted, and the air was fresh and sharp with the scent of the snow.

Lights brightened Jane's windows on the first floor, the second floor dark but for a single dim light from a window he was pretty sure was a bathroom. Even from the opposite side of the road, Dom could hear Ben inside talking in a steady stream about something to do with his games. When the kid was interested in something, he could really talk. Dom smiled.

The very faint sound of Jane's voice drew him to her front yard. He couldn't hear what she was saying exactly, but her tone was amused and patient and content. If Dom knocked on her door, that amused contentment would vanish.

He almost walked away.

Instead, he climbed the wooden steps up to her front porch and rang the bell. The ding-dong sound silenced the conversation.

Jane's scent hit Dom hard, even through the barrier of the door, and he had to brace himself for the sight of her. She looked beautiful, framed in a soft halo by the entryway light behind her. Her dark hair hung loose past her shoulders in thick waves, free from the bun she usually wore to work. He flexed his fingers when the thought of running his hands through her hair almost had him reaching for her. There were faint circles under her dark eyes, but the creases that showed occasionally at the corners were relaxed. She wore a simple pair of fitted jeans and a long-sleeved plaid button down over a snug white t-shirt. Casual, stunning, and perfect, as far as Dom was concerned. He just wished he could tell her without making her uncomfortable.

She stood in the doorway facing him, her expression hard to read, her scent full of the complicated mix of denial and desire that drove Dom crazy.

"Can we talk?" he asked.

From the living room, Ben called out, "It's cold."

"Sorry," Jane called back. To Dom, she said, "Let's talk outside." She grabbed her coat off the coat rack behind the door, then motioned him to the porch railing.

He waited until she'd pulled a hat and gloves from the pockets of her thick snow coat and put them on, wanting her to be comfortable and a little worried the cold air would chill her before they finished. Since he knew she wouldn't accept his embrace, and his significantly warmer body heat, he stood with his hands in his pockets to keep from pulling her into his arms.

"You sure you'll be warm enough?" he asked.

"I'm fine. What did you want to talk about?"

He hesitated a few seconds before deciding to dive straight to the point. "I know it's not my business, but I want to know why you keep turning me away. You can't say you don't want me. I know you do. You know I want you."

She sucked in a sharp breath but remained quiet.

"I realize you don't like to talk about your past. And I know I've no right to demand answers. But I want some anyway. After that kiss, I can't go on like we've been for the last six years."

She pursed her lips and looked away from him, out over the street. It took all of Dom's willpower not to step closer or make any move that might draw her out of her reverie. His hands fisted in his pockets as he held his position, waiting for her to make a decision.

He watched that decision flow through her body, her shoulders straightening, the deep breath she took and held for a half second before letting it out on a long sigh. She looked at him from the corner of her eye, then settled her hands on the porch railing and kept her gaze on her gloves.

"You're right about me not liking to bring up my past. You're also right that it's none of your business. But…it's only fair to tell you the story." She sighed again. "It's just, see, I've made some very bad choices over the years. All of them to do with men." Her lips lifted in a faint smile and she half met his gaze. "I have terrible taste in men."

He raised his brows in mock offense. She grinned and that made the ache in his chest ease a little.

"Ben's father… Well, I'm sure Nick told you the man knocked me around sometimes."

Dom's fists tightened, his nails biting into the palms of his hands. He didn't otherwise flinch or move. "He didn't actually. Tiana mentioned it once, but said she didn't know the full story."

Jane snorted. "I don't tell it. Just the short version. Eirene's good for that, you know. No one digs if you're not willing to tell."

He did flinch at that. Because he was digging, because he'd come here asking for answers she didn't want to give.

"I wasn't married to the man," she continued, her gaze once again on her hands around the porch railing, "but we lived together. I ran off with him when I was seventeen. My parents were strict and controlling. I wanted my freedom, and Larry gave me that. At first. I was so young…" She shook her head. "Anyway, it started out all romantic and rebellious. My parents disowned me, and I thought even that was romantic. Kids are such idiots. Larry and I lived in a trailer, me waiting tables, him looking for odd jobs."

"Where?"

"Nebraska. First time he hit me, I was too surprised to argue. And too in love to realize I should be mad. He was good at convincing me it was my fault. Every time. Most of them are, you know? The men who hit. Very good at convincing us it's our fault. And for some damned reason, we all buy it." She shook herself hard, as if shaking off her feelings. "Then Ben came along, and we were a happy little family for a few months. Larry didn't hit me for…well, a while. He started again when Ben was around a year. By the time Ben was two, it was obvious he was different. And Larry's patience with the baby was wearing thin. I knew he'd start hitting Ben soon."

She faced Dom. "That I couldn't have. Whatever might be done to me, I refused to let anyone hurt my baby. I left and took Ben with me the day after the pediatrician told me he was probably autistic."

"Did Larry look for you?"

"Na. Not sure he cared, honestly. Which is kind of surprising in hindsight. But he was already calling Ben awful names…" She pressed her lips together and glanced back at the house.

"Does Ben know any of this?" Dom asked very quietly.

"Only that his father wasn't a very nice man and we had to leave. I had trouble telling him even that much. Ben's very sensitive to my moods and feelings. Talking about his father got me so upset it upset him. Better for all of us just not to talk about it."

"I shouldn't have asked…"

"No, no. It's okay. You should know this."

"I'm not like Larry, you know. I would never hit a woman."

She waved that away. "I know. The logical part of my brain does anyway. But the part of me that wants you…"

Hearing her admit that out loud for the first time sent a shock of pain and need through Dom, sharper than anything he'd experienced before this. Without thinking, he took a step closer to her but stopped, knowing she'd turn away any physical contact. Dom didn't even know this Larry, and he wanted to kill him for the things he'd done to Jane.

She nodded over her shoulder to the house. "Ben was worth going through everything I did with Larry. I wouldn't have my baby if I hadn't given up my parents and run away. So I don't regret it. Not one little bit. Which means I can't really consider Larry a mistake, even if he wasn't a very healthy decision."

"There's more."

She half-smiled. "Smart man. I knew that, too." She pulled in a deep breath. "Yes. More bad choices. Some stupid decisions. All of them to do with men. Kept picking losers, every one. A boss who fired me when I ended our fling. A trucker who told me to abandon Ben and run away with him." She rolled her eyes. "I was always attracted to that rebel-without-a-cause type, the strong, sexy loner, and it bit me in the ass every time. The worst, though, was right before Ben and I moved back to Eirene."

He knew from previous conversations that she'd been in Eirene with Ben for a short period of time, moved on to Kansas City where a cousin had offered to give Ben the speech therapy he needed for free, and when Ben was able to communicate at almost age level, she'd moved back to Eirene. She had never told him much about her time in Kansas City beyond the work she and her cousin did with Ben. Anything personal beyond Ben, she'd kept to herself.

"That man," she said, "he was a real mistake. A married man." She met his gaze. "I had no idea when I started up with him. I would never mess around with a married man. I might make bad choices, but that was a rule I stuck to. Bastard. When I found out, I told him off and tried to leave. He begged and pleaded. Then he hit me."

Dom's jaw tightened and his muscles bunched for a fight. The reaction was instinctive and instantaneous.

"It had been years since I'd let a man raise his hand to me," she went on, not noticing Dom's reaction. "And he caught me by surprise. Didn't think he had it in him. I thought he was a nice guy. Sweet and gentle. I went for him *because* I thought he was different from all the other men I'd been with." She shrugged. "He was very responsible and stable. A safe choice. I was so stunned when he hit me, I didn't react right away. Guess he took that as a sign to hit me again."

"Where were you? Was Ben around?" Dom heard the growl in his voice and tried clearing his throat. It didn't help. His tiger was so angry, he was having trouble convincing it the incident was in the past.

"I never let the men I was seeing around Ben. No, we were at a hotel. Fancy one, too." She grimaced. "Really thought I'd found a good man that time. He hit me twice more before I thought of Ben and started hitting back. It crossed my mind the married bastard could kill me, and then who would take care of my baby? Ben needed me, a lot. I couldn't abide the thought of leaving him on his own. So I started screaming and fighting and cursing and…" She snorted. "Years of anger came roaring out. When the room's door opened, I thought for sure it was the hotel management and the cops and I was going to jail. Turned out to be the man's wife."

"Shit. What happened?"

"Apparently, she'd heard me screaming about him being a liar and not telling me he was married. When she saw my split lip and half-closed eye, she had her husband arrested for assault."

"She did?" Dom wouldn't have been more surprised if she'd told him the wife was blue. "She took your side?"

Jane smiled, the first real, full smile he'd seen from her tonight.

"Turned out," she said, "Grace Lancaster was super rich and thought she'd married for love. But he'd cheated a couple of times and was on his last warning. The hitting women wasn't a new thing either, so she believed I'd been defending myself even though he claimed I'd started it all."

"So what happened in the end?"

"She made sure he did jail time, then she paid me off to keep the story out of the papers."

"Paid you off?"

"Enough money that I could move back to Eirene. Ben's best friend had just moved, he was sad, I was beat up —literally and figuratively—and ready for a change. We both missed Eirene." Jane paused, her expression distant. "Grace is a real nice woman. Learned about Ben's autism and started a college fund for him."

"The wife of a man you were sleeping with gave you the money to send Ben to college?"

"I know. Sounds ridiculous. But there you go. She's a good person who has bad taste in men, too. We understand each other." She chuckled softly. "She's one of my best friends now. Still lives in Kansas City, but we talk all the time. She comes to visit when she can. I keep trying to talk her into moving here. She'd fit right in."

Pulling in a deep breath, Jane faced Dom fully. "When Ben and I got to Eirene again, I swore I'd never let another man into my life. I can't trust myself, you see. I make bad choices. If I'm attracted to a man, it's always been a warning sign. And I can't afford to keep making the same mistakes anymore. For my sake. For Ben's."

"Ben's growing up and at college. He'll be on his own soon. Maybe here, maybe somewhere else. Then what will you do?"

"I'll enjoy my life in a town I love. A full life, too, I might add. I've got friends, a great job, my volunteer work at the daycare center. I'm almost done with my MBA, and Nick and I are already talking about me taking a bigger role at the diner."

"You're working on an MBA?" Nick hadn't mentioned that to Dom, but the memory of the business book on her coffee table came back to him.

"Turns out I have quite the head for business," she said, pride clear in her voice. "And numbers. Guess Ben got that from me. I'm even considering starting my own business one day, probably something to do with kids. Anyway, as you can see, I'm enjoying every minute of my life, Dom. I don't need a man to make me happy."

"Fair enough. But I could make you happier."

She swallowed visibly at that. "I can't trust myself,

Dom. I have never, not once made a good decision about a man."

"I'm not like those other men. I'm not married. I'd never ask you to abandon Ben. I *like* Ben. And I would never, ever hurt you."

"But there's violence in you. You're no stranger to a fight. I can see it. I saw it today when you and Nick sent those thugs away."

He sighed. "Me and my brothers…we had to fight growing up. We had no choice if we wanted to survive. We got good at it so we didn't have to fight very often."

"You are good at it, though." It wasn't a question.

"I only hit bad people," he said with a scowl.

She laughed. "There's a line in a movie something like that."

"Jane…"

"It's not your fault. I'm drawn to that part of you. You're a dangerous man, somewhere deep inside."

"But I'd never be dangerous to you."

"You are dangerous to me already. Because I want you so much."

He took another involuntary step toward her at that, but stopped and kept his hands in his pockets by sheer willpower.

"But I can't risk it," she finished. "I'm attracted to your danger, your edge. And I can't…be with someone who speaks to that part of me."

"Can't you just see me as a computer geek? Nice and harmless?"

She laughed, the sound sharp and loud in the quiet

night. He grinned at the reaction even though his heart hurt from her rejection.

She cupped his cheek in one hand and shook her head. "You might be nice, but you are certainly not harmless."

"I wouldn't be another bad choice," he murmured, no longer able to keep his distance. He didn't touch her, he kept his hands in his pockets, but he did lean in, putting his mouth very close to hers. "I'd make sure you were happy, Jane. I'd never hurt you."

When she didn't move away, he kissed her, slow and gentle at first, lingering over the softness of her lips, the heady flavor of her scent filling him. His hands still in his pockets, he pressed his body against hers, giving her the room to move away if she wanted to, growling with satisfaction when she didn't. He tasted her, savored her, showed her with his kiss what he couldn't convince her of with words.

And then he eased away, before she could stop him, before she could do anything to break the magic of the moment.

"Please," he said, "think about giving me a chance. Don't say yes or no now. Just…consider it." He stepped off the porch. "Tell Ben I said hi. I'll see you tomorrow."

Jane stayed in the cold on the porch, staring into the darkness for a long time after Dom left, considering what he'd said, shocked by how much she wanted to give in. Well, maybe not that shocked. Her body was humming from yet another knee-melting kiss. She could only imagine what his delectable mouth would do to the rest of her if she finally took him to bed.

Until Dom, she'd been sure she'd never want another man in her life. He'd changed everything, and part of her resented him for that. Getting involved was a risk, a huge one for her. One she didn't *want* to take again.

Her past decisions taunted her.

But Dom was a good man. He had a good family behind him. Ben adored him. Dom adored Ben. Dom had never shown her anything but kindness and patience…

A memory of that morning on Main Street with Dom and his brothers facing off against the thugs flashed through her mind—the way Dom had looked, serious and very dangerous, but fully in control. The way he'd pushed that one man away from Nick, firmly and with surprising ease.

He might be a nice man, but he was strong and easy with violence. A lot easier than he wanted to admit. She didn't know the full story behind his and his brothers' past, but she'd picked up enough from Nick to know they'd fought a lot as kids. She'd learned from their aunt Alexis that they'd had a pretty rough life for a few years. There *was* violence there, in Dom's eyes, in the way his muscles bunched whenever she admitted someone had hurt her…

When her stomach danced in a giddy little thrill at the thought of his protective gesture, she groaned. Damn it all to hell, she hadn't changed a bit. Grace was wrong about her. She hadn't learned a damned thing. She *was* still looking for a protector. All of the mistakes over all the years had come down to her running toward some big strong man to keep her safe, first from her parents, then from the insecurity of her life. She'd kept looking for a rescuer.

But Grace had been right about one thing. Jane didn't fucking need that. She could keep herself safe. She *had* kept herself safe…relatively speaking…for years. And she'd kept Ben safe. Her life now was settled and secure. And *she'd* made it that way. She was happy, damn it. She didn't need a man.

But God help her, she wanted one—Dom. Only him.

She rolled her eyes. She was too old for this shit, for crushes and this lusty thrill at the hint of danger she saw in a man. Too old to be looking for a *hero*. Too damned old to be pining after something so bad for her. If she could resist a daily slice of chocolate cake, she should be able to resist Dom.

She stalked back inside, stamping her boots off on the rug outside the door with more force than was absolutely necessary, cursing under her breath as she closed the door behind her…

Trying not to hear the little voice in the back of her mind whispering that Dom wasn't bad for her. Dom might actually be very good for her.

F rom the shadows behind a small clump of trees half a block from the waitress' house, Frank watched the tiger leave after laying a solid kiss on the bitch. So, that was the asshole's weakness—a human woman.

Easy prey.

He watched the human until she went back inside, then he glanced at his watch. His alpha and beta were meeting with the tiger brothers in another couple of hours. Perfect timing. He smiled into the dark, his gaze returning to the human woman's door. Time for a little party.

CHAPTER SIX

The Walsh brothers arrived at Nick's diner precisely on time, well after Main Street had quieted and the diner had closed. Late enough that the townspeople of Eirene weren't likely to notice the clandestine meeting.

Nick had refused to have the wolves in his home, and Dom couldn't blame him. All three of the Chernikov brothers were protective of Tiana and Chrissy, too protective to let the wolves near them. But the diner was also Nick's territory, which put the wolves at a disadvantage. Given the circumstances, it was more appropriate than the neutral ground they might otherwise use.

Dom had met Adam Walsh, the pack beta, but this was the first time he'd come face-to-face with the alpha. Gabriel Walsh looked a lot like his brother, about the same height as Nick, with dark hair that was almost black and blue eyes. His features were a little longer and narrower than Adam's, but otherwise, the family resemblance was obvious.

Nick got everyone seated at one of the round open tables in the middle of the dining room, the three Chernikovs sitting opposite the two werewolves. Nick offered drinks, which were rejected all around, then got right down to business.

"The deal we made was no wolf trouble in my town and you could open your businesses in my territory. We're having wolf trouble in my town."

"They aren't harming any humans," Gabriel said.

"Wolf arguments could lead to human casualties. We all know that."

"You're bringing in a huge number of tigers. We haven't objected."

"It's my territory. And they don't live here. They also won't hurt anyone in this town. Eirene is mine. I'll defend it. And not with money this time."

Dom didn't show any reaction to Nick's threat, but he wanted to growl in agreement. He'd be here to fight with Nick if necessary. So would Mitch. The Chernikov brothers stood together in all things.

And at some point in the last six years, Dom had come to think of Eirene as a kind of home—one he didn't visit often, but a home nonetheless. Jane lived here. Ben lived here when he wasn't at college. Any threat to them was a threat he'd put down.

"We'll keep the others out," Adam said, stepping into the tension between the alpha and Nick.

Nick didn't look away from Gabriel when he said, "You're having some internal fighting. I don't need the details. I don't even want them. But that infighting needs to remain in your territory. For all our sakes."

Gabriel's lips pressed together in a tight line. He glanced at Adam. Adam shrugged. Gabriel took a deep breath and faced Nick again. "Are you asking Siobhan to close her shop here?"

"Not yet," Nick said. "But I will if it becomes necessary."

"She employs a lot of people."

"I can give them all temporary jobs until a new business moves in."

"You have an answer for everything?"

"When it comes to Eirene, yes."

Mitch huffed out a laugh. Adam narrowed his eyes at Mitch. Mitch smiled back. With a lot of teeth.

Dom rolled his eyes. His baby brother was known for being the charming Chernikov. But only when he wanted to be.

"There's no need for tension between us," Adam said, breaking eye contact with Mitch first—a wolf sign of backing down. "We all want the same things. Peaceful homes, prosperous businesses, and no issues for or from the humans."

Gabriel ran a hand through his hair and the tension in his shoulders eased. "I'm sorry about the trouble," he finally said. "The infighting is... Well, some of the converted wolves in the pack liked the way our former alpha did things."

"Running the pack into the ground financially?" Nick asked.

"They didn't know about that. They liked the badass, fear-no-one bullshit Chris peddled. Most of the ones we're having trouble with joined the pack in the last few years of Chris' father's reign. They don't know what it's supposed to be like in a pack."

"Is it just the converted wolves?" Dom asked.

Werewolves were one of the species of shifters that could turn humans. Tigers couldn't—which was part of the reason their extinction problems were so complicated. As far as Dom knew, it took a really strong werewolf alpha to even manage the conversion, and they tried not to do it often in stable packs. He seemed to remember hearing that most of the conversions these days were done by rogue wolves who lived outside pack structure.

The one thing he did know was if the wrong kind of human was turned, a very dangerous werewolf emerged. If this pack had a lot of them, there was a reason for it. And even more potential danger.

Adam and Gabriel exchanged another long look before Gabriel gestured for Adam to speak.

"Some of the older pack members," Adam said, "the ones who felt stifled under Doug Corwin and free under his son Chris are feeding the chaos. Most of the pack wants stability. Most preferred the way things were under Doug's reign and want that again. But it only takes a few to cause trouble."

"How many converted wolves do you have?" Nick asked. "Chris didn't seem strong enough to turn a human."

"He wasn't," Adam said. "We took in strays—under Doug's orders. He felt sorry for them, since most of them hadn't made a choice to change." Adam waved off the story. "Anyway, we have more than is typical in a pack, but not too many that we can't handle them."

"And we'll ensure they keep their machinations out of Eirene," Gabriel added. "Siobhan loves her boutique. She's doing really well and so is the fruit and vegetable market we opened here. All of it's helping the entire pack."

"The townsfolks here like Siobhan and her shop so I'd hate to see it close, too," Nick said. "I'm all for a stable pack as my neighbors." He leaned back in his seat, losing some of the territorial bluster when he asked, "Can we help?"

Adam smiled. "Thanks for the offer. We'll sort it out."

Before Nick could say more, Dom's phone buzzed. He had it on vibrate but glanced at the screen just in case. When he saw Jane's house number pop up, he frowned and answered.

"Dom, Dom, Dom..." Ben sounded breathless and panicked.

Dom was on his feet, already moving for the door. "Ben, what's wrong?"

"Mom. He took her. Don't know where. Help..."

Dom was running, moving at shifter speed before Ben could finish his sentence, tearing across town to Jane's house so fast he would have looked like a blur to any human who'd seen him.

He wasn't even a little surprised that Mitch and Nick followed him.

Ben was still stuttering through the phone when Dom knocked on the door. "Ben, that's me at the door. Open up."

He sniffed the area on the porch and near the door, looking for clues, and caught the scent of the wolf he'd confronted in town that morning, the one Jane had been worried about. Frank.

Dom was mid-growl when Ben opened the door.

His eyes were wide and his pale skin so white it was almost translucent. "Dom, he took her. He took her."

Ben wouldn't meet Dom's gaze—his eye contact got sketchier when he was upset. That sign of his distress hit Dom right in the gut, tearing at his heart, almost equal to the panic he felt for Jane.

"Nick," Dom said, facing his older brother, "stay with Ben. Keep him safe." To Ben, he said, "I'll get her back, Ben. I swear I will. Stay in the house. I'll take care of it. How long has your mom been missing?"

"Just now." He met Dom's gaze briefly. "You got here fast."

Dom nodded, almost smiling but too worried for the expression to stick. He took another deep breath, pulling in the necessary information, then jogged back to the street, following Jane's scent. The fact that her fear lingered in her scent and that the fear mixed with the bastard wolf's scent made Dom's tiger roar.

The wolf and Jane's trail moved into the trees, away from the streets of Eirene and into the deep woods, toward the direction of the pack's territory. Dom barely cleared the trees before he let his tiger out, shifting so fast his clothes shredded and his body actually trembled for a moment as he dropped onto all fours. Then he was running—Mitch, still in human form, a solid and welcome presence at his side.

In his tiger form, the scent trail was easier to follow. The wolf hadn't tried to disguise himself at all, like he intended for Dom to show up.

What little of Dom's logic was left through his anger and fear thought, *Be careful what you wish for, wolf.*

Jane grunted and cursed as the thug pushed her against a tree. He'd carried her over his shoulder through the woods, at speeds that were scary unnatural. She was so disoriented and terrified, it took all she had just to keep her feet under her.

Ben. Ben would be so worried. God, what if her boy tried to come help her. He knew the woods around Eirene well, but the thought of him anywhere near the bastard who'd taken her made her every maternal instinct panic. *No, Ben. Please stay home. Call the sheriff. Don't leave the house.*

The thug cast a brief glance at her. "Stay there, bitch. Or I'll kill you."

She glared but didn't answer. Unfortunately, she had no doubt the sonofabitch could kill her, but she wasn't going to just hang around and wait for that to happen. She stayed where she was, but studied her surroundings and the sky overhead, trying to get her bearings.

The asshole paced back and forth in front of her, reminding Jane of a caged animal. Every so often, he'd raise his head and pull in a deep breath, as if smelling for something.

Jane shivered. And not just from cold.

But she was freezing from the weather, too. The snow in this part of the woods was thick and untrampled. The tree she'd been tossed against had a little space under it without snow, but the ground under her feet was like ice. She had a flannel shirt over her t-shirt, and socks but no boots. No coat. Even if she got away from the bastard, she was way outside of town, nowhere near a road, in the dead of night in the middle of winter.

She was so screwed.

Ben needed her. She had to figure a way out of this. For Ben. No dying yet.

She wrapped her arms around her stomach, trying to stay as warm as she could as she looked for an escape route. Suddenly, the thug's head came up, his gaze turning toward the trees in the direction Jane thought they'd come.

A moment later, a flash of white plowed into the thug at chest height, sending him and the white blur flying into a pine.

When the two separated, Jane almost screamed at the sight of a huge, white tiger standing in front of the crouched man, the animal's open mouth revealing a scary set of very large, very sharp teeth. She choked on her shock and the scream bubbled up, but she was so terrified it came out as a gasping squeak.

Her brain had barely registered the presence of a tiger —a fucking tiger!—when something the size of a large, misshapen dog charged from deeper in the trees, hitting the side of the tiger and sending them both into a tumbling heap.

The thug laughed, stood and snarled at the tiger. "I knew you'd come for her. Think you can take on two of us, kitty?"

Jane blinked a few times, sure she was seeing things when the thug's body started to convulse, then…things happened, things out of a nightmare, things she couldn't even name, they were so horrific. But the sounds, the popping and ripping, the crunching and the blood. The thug shouted as if in pain, folding and collapsing to the ground, looking like his skin was trying to crawl off his body.

She nearly threw up. She wasn't sure why she didn't, because her stomach heaved and everything in her screamed that what she was seeing wasn't possible. She was having a nightmare. She wasn't actually watching a man split open and break apart right before her eyes.

She couldn't even look away. Some weird self-preservation instinct kept her from closing her eyes. But she knew there were nightmares coming her way now, nightmares she'd live with for a long time.

Oh, Charlie had warned them all… They all knew but… Seeing was a very different prospect.

Werewolves. Jesus H. Christ.

When something landed on her shoulder, she finally did

scream and whipped around to face the source. Mitch Chernikov stood there, looking solid and real and...not at all surprised by the tiger and the giant dog-thing she was pretty sure was a werewolf and the man tearing apart from the inside out.

"Are you okay?" he asked. "Are you hurt?"

"Cold," she said, her teeth chattering now—though she had a feeling this was more from shock than the snow. "What the hell, Mitch? Am I hallucinating?"

"No." He looked grim as he stared at the scene beyond her.

She kept her gaze on him, afraid to look. Afraid that she wasn't looking.

"I need you to stay here, out of the way, okay?" Mitch said, holding her gaze. "We can handle them. But he's going to have a hard time concentrating if he thinks you're in danger. He'll get hurt if he doesn't focus on the others. Okay?"

"Who?" She shook her head. "What are you talking about?"

"The tiger. Just...don't get in his way."

"Damn straight I won't. What the hell is a fucking tiger doing in Colorado?"

"Long story. I'll let him explain. Just keep safe. We'll take care of the rest."

"Wait..."

But Mitch was already moving toward the growls and snarls that were filling the area. She didn't dare keep her back to all those noises now and turned to face the scene. To her horror, two more of the werewolves were circling the tiger who'd hunkered down in a crouch, waiting without looking like he was watching the wolves.

She kept her back to the pine tree, her heart pounding hard enough to hurt, breathing so fast she was afraid she'd pass out if she couldn't slow things down.

She almost screamed again when Mitch walked right up to one of the wolves. She opened her mouth to call out, to warn him, but the wolf launched, so fast she barely saw the movement.

Mitch moved too, but she knew he couldn't be fast enough…

And then the wolf was flying over Mitch's head and into a tree. Mitch rose from his half-crouch and smiled at the wolf, as if he was having fun.

In the next instant, the tiger flowed into motion, and her eyes couldn't follow. The white animal seemed to be in two places at once, first flipping one wolf into the air, then swatting another hard into a tree.

The fight was an awful, awesome thing to witness. Everything moved so fast, she really couldn't see much more than blurs in the darkness. One moment, the glowing white of the tiger's fur showed up in one place, a blink later the tiger was in another area entirely. Mitch moved just as fast, shocking Jane with his speed. And the wolves…dark, hulking shapes under the trees… The only ways she could spot them in the midst of the fight was when one faced her and she got a good look at their glowing yellow eyes.

The only thing she could tell from all the roaring and shouting, hissing and growling, the sound of tree bark crunching and the yelps of pain, was that it looked like

Mitch and the tiger were winning. They fought against three huge werewolves and were winning. From the look of Mitch's grin, when he paused long enough for her to see him clearly, they might even be winning easily.

How the hell was any of this possible in the real world?

She almost didn't react when two more huge hairy beasts lunged into the mix. It was too much for any sane person to take, too overwhelming to process. So the fact that the new wolves didn't attack the tiger or Mitch but instead went after the other three wolves took her several moments to recognize.

There was a lot of snarling now, the three original werewolves backing down under the presence of the two new ones.

Well, that was interesting.

A sound like a branch cracking disrupted her fascinated study of the wolves. She looked up in time to see one of the pine trees, young but still big, start to buckle and fall—right toward her.

She leapt to one side, tripping and scrambling over the needle and snow-covered ground in her stocking feet, trying to get out of the way of the falling tree. She looked back, knew some of the branches were going to catch her, and scrambled faster...only to get hit by something much larger than a tree branch.

The wind whooshed out of her, and she instinctively wrapped her arms around the thing that had barreled into her and rolled her beyond the falling tree. Soft fur tickled her palms.

Their roll stopped at the base of another tree. Jane

blinked up at the sky for several long moments as she forced her lungs to take in air again. Then she focused on the huge white tiger looming over her. She held perfectly still, but a trembling started in her limbs that she couldn't control. And when the tiger dipped its head close to her face, she closed her eyes tight, some animal part of her brain recognizing that she was about to become cat food.

A rough, wet lap of a tongue dampened her cheek. She squinted open one eye as the tiger nudged her cheek gently with his warm nose. She blinked. The animal was looking her right in the eyes, staring at her…

Those eyes.

Before she could fully understand what she was seeing, Mitch was there helping her to her feet as the tiger backed away, settled on its haunches, and watched her.

"Did the tiger just save me from the tree?" she asked Mitch.

"Yes."

"Is that Dom?" She wasn't even sure why she had that crazy thought. Where it had come from. Or why she was convinced of the truth of it with every fiber of her being.

"It is," Mitch said with a sigh.

"You all have a lot of explaining to do."

"Suppose so."

"Where's Ben?" Thoughts of her son suddenly pushed all her terror and confusion to the side. "He called you?"

"He called Dom. Nick is with him. He's safe in your house."

She looked back at the wolves. "Never thought I'd actually see one," she muttered. "What happens now?"

"They'll be taken care of," Mitch said, hesitantly, as if he wasn't sure how much to say.

"Werewolves," she muttered. "That's the only problem with Eirene, you know. All the damned werewolves."

Mitch stared at her with his eyebrows raised, his mouth hanging open just a bit. The tiger made a chuffing noise that sounded suspiciously like a laugh to Jane.

"We have a *lot* to talk about," she said to the tiger. Then to Mitch, "I need to get home and see to Ben. He'll be going out of his mind. This kind of thing…" She didn't even want to think about her baby being worried or how he'd react to this. She just knew she needed to get back to him and make sure he was okay.

"We can leave," Mitch said. "We're a ways outside of town though. You want me to carry you?" He nodded down to her feet.

She glared at her soaking wet socks, her toes numb from the cold. Then she frowned up at Mitch. "Where the hell's your coat?"

He grinned. "We left in too much of a hurry to stop for coats."

She glanced back at the tiger that was supposedly Dom. "You look warm enough."

He nodded in agreement. The show of understanding made her heart thump.

"You can ride on his back, if you think you'll be warmer," Mitch offered, gesturing to the tiger. "But if you're not ready for that, I'll carry you. I can move pretty fast. We'll be back to your house before the real chill sinks in."

"I saw a little of that speed earlier. You a tiger, too?"

He shrugged. "It'll be quicker if one of us carries you."

"Ah hell." She put her hands on her hips and stared at the snow under her feet even as her toes started to protest the freeze by sending shooting pains up her legs. "Fine. How?"

To her surprise, Mitch just leaned down and picked her up, one arm under her legs, the other behind her back, carrying her as if she weighed nothing at all.

The tiger rose to his feet and his eyes narrowed. He made a low growling sound, his lips lifting in a slight snarl.

"Easy, Dom," Mitch said. "You'll scare her. She's like a sister to me, no need to get all growly."

"Why's he growling at you?" Jane asked.

"Jealousy," Mitch said. "Hold tight. This is going to be disorienting."

"The wolves…" She looked back but to her surprise all five of the huge beasts were gone. She hadn't even heard them go. "Are they…?"

She never got the question out. In the next moment, Mitch started running, the jolt shocking her, the speed making her stomach drop, the sight of the trees blurring past making her nauseas. She caught sight of the white tiger keeping pace and then had to close her eyes or risk throwing up.

CHAPTER SEVEN

Jane was only a little surprised when Tiana opened her front door just as Mitch stopped on the porch. Jane's stomach was turning from the speed of the run, and her limbs felt like ice, but they'd gotten home so quickly, she barely had time to worry about frostbite. Mitch set her on her feet, and Tiana immediately wrapped her up in a hug.

"Are you okay?" Tiana said. "You must be freezing. Come on inside. Ben is fine. He's in the living room with Nick."

The fact that Tiana answered Jane's first question without Jane having to ask made Jane smile. Woman had definitely become a mother. Jane glanced back at the white tiger that was supposed to be Dom and frowned. The neighborhood was going to be getting an eyeful if anyone was awake to see this.

"You better get inside, looking like that," Jane said. "Don't scare Ben."

She didn't wait on Dom to follow her order, just hurried in, her cold skin stinging in the warmth of her home, and headed right to Ben.

He leapt off the couch and threw his arms around her, his hug so tight it nearly choked her. She didn't care. She returned the hug fiercely.

"I was scared," Ben muttered against her neck. "Didn't know what to do."

"You did exactly the right thing, baby. I'm okay. Don't worry now. I'm fine."

"Dom saved you?"

"And Mitch. They scared off the bad guys."

"Good." He pulled back, not quite meeting her eyes. "Bad guys? I'm not twelve."

She snorted, all the tension of the last hour easing. Behind it, her body felt like rubber—stinging rubber as her skin warmed. She cupped Ben's cheek in one hand.

He frowned. "You're cold. I'll get you a blanket. Sit on the couch."

She was reluctant to let him go, but she could tell he needed to be helpful. "Could you bring me some dry socks, too?"

He nodded as he hurried from the living room. She watched him go, her heart aching a little. Her baby was growing up. But he was still her baby.

She blinked away the sentiment and faced Nick as she pulled off her soaked socks. Her toes stung like crazy. "Thanks for staying with him. Was he very upset?"

"Of course," Nick said. "But he handled it well. He paced a lot, and pulled at his fingers, but otherwise kept it together."

She nodded back at Dom who was slinking into the living room. He'd obviously hidden somewhere so Ben wouldn't see him. Nick's eyes widened just a bit and he exchanged a look with Mitch and Tiana.

"You a tiger, too?" Jane asked Nick.

He sighed and shrugged.

She took that as a yes. Turning to Tiana, she said, "You, too?"

"Yes."

"And your baby?"

"Yes."

"She changes now?"

"Not until she's around three."

"Will it hurt her?"

"Not any more than falling on her butt as she learns to walk. It's natural to us. It doesn't hurt."

"Sure as hell looked like it hurt when the werewolf changed."

"Jesus," Nick said. "He shifted in front of you? Sonofabitch."

"Where did the tiger come from?" Ben asked as he came back into the living room.

Jane jumped and spun to face him. "He's…"

Ben handed her a blanket as he took in the room. "Oh, it's Dom. Hi, Dom."

For a very long time, everyone in the room just stared at Ben in silence. This made Ben so uncomfortable, he started pulling on his fingers again. Jane snapped out of her shock first and waved at everyone so they'd stop staring. That kind of attention always upset Ben.

"Why do you think that's Dom?" she asked.

"He's the only one missing," Ben said in a matter-of-fact way, like that answer was obvious.

"You're not…scared?" Jane asked.

"It's Dom." As if that answered the question.

"Well, there you go." Jane jerked her hands in the air, giving in to Ben's logic. Then she swung the blanket around her shoulders and sat on the couch to slip on the fluffy socks Ben handed her. Ben snugged up next to her when she was done. She wrapped her arm around him, keeping him close.

"Who's with your baby?" she asked Tiana.

"My parents arrived this afternoon. They're looking after her. I'll have to get back soon, but…I'm assuming you have questions?"

"I do. But you can go if you need to." Jane narrowed her eyes at the three brothers. "They can do the answering."

Tiana smiled, though she tried to hide it, and flashed Nick another look. "I brought spare clothes, just in case." She nodded at Dom. "The bag's in the hall. It's all Nick's stuff but should be big enough for you."

"So your clothes don't just magically shift with you?" Jane asked. She raised her brows at Dom, realizing if he changed now, he'd be naked and maybe she might like the idea of Dom naked a little too much. "You can use the bigger bathroom upstairs," she told him.

She didn't want to watch him shift. Seeing the wolf

change had been enough for one night. Even the thought of Dom naked couldn't quite erase the horror of that.

"I like white tigers," Ben said after Dom left the room.

"Do you?" Jane asked. "Since when?"

"Always. They're pretty."

She smiled. "Tell Dom he's pretty when he comes back out. It'll be good for him."

"Okay."

She hugged Ben tighter, then faced Mitch and Nick who were shuffling from foot to foot, looking distinctly uncomfortable.

"Sit," she ordered. "I'm too tired to keep looking up at you."

Nick settled into a chair, and Mitch made himself comfortable on the floor in front of the fireplace, his back to the low flames. Nick or Tiana must have started the fire. Since Jane was still trying to warm up, she was grateful for it. In fact, she kind of envied Mitch's place in front of it. Except that she didn't want to be anywhere but right at Ben's side at the moment.

She'd managed to keep almost all of the bad things that had happened to her over the years from Ben. Ben didn't even know how bad his own father had been, though he did know the man wasn't particularly nice. For the first time in eighteen years, her son had come face-to-face with the worst the world had to offer. And she hated that more than just about anything else that had happened that night.

She considered sending him up to bed so he wouldn't have to hear about were-tigers and werewolves and all the other scary things she'd be asking the Chernikovs about.

But he'd taken to Dom being a tiger so well, she decided it was best he knew everything. Knowing would, hopefully, help keep him safe.

They waited in silence until Dom came back into the room. He was dressed in a pair of sweat pants that were just a little too short for him, and a t-shirt that fit a little tight. He was only a couple inches taller than Nick, but also just a little thicker. Obviously it made a difference in how the clothes fit.

Dom's borrowed clothes showed off all the beautiful male muscles she'd long admired. Now that she knew what it felt like to have that gorgeous body pressed up against hers, she had a harder time ignoring how good he looked in a tight t-shirt. His hair was mussed, like he'd just woken up. But his eyes were bright and alert. And leery. His jaw was tight and his shoulders stiff.

So he was worried about how she'd take this tiger business? Well, he should be. She'd known there was violence in him. This wasn't what she'd been expecting, exactly, but it was a confirmation of all her worst fears. Her taste in men was horrible.

He saved you. Twice.

She ignored the reminder from her conscience. She didn't want to consider that she'd finally found a man who could protect her, because she didn't need a protector. Even if he had rescued her tonight.

She pushed away the conflicting emotions to focus on the tiger thing. "Okay, start talking. I knew there were werewolves in Colorado. Never seen one go from human to wolf before. That was pretty awful." She caught Dom's wince from the corner of her eye as he settled in the seat next to Ben's side of the couch.

"How long have you known about the wolves?" Nick asked.

"Since that gang of them harassed the town just before you arrived. Charlie spread the word."

"Charlie knew?"

"Course. He's lived here for nearly a hundred years. You think he'd miss something like werewolf neighbors?"

Mitch chuckled at that. "I knew I liked old Charlie."

Dom threw his little brother a quelling look. Mitch just grinned back and shrugged.

"So…you knew this whole time?" Nick asked. "I thought everyone assumed they were a motorcycle gang?"

"We did. A motorcycle gang of werewolves."

"Why didn't you tell me?"

"We all assumed you knew. You did get them to leave us alone. Figured you had to know what they really were. Plus you've heard Charlie telling stories about the beasts in the woods. What did you think he was talking about?"

"I thought he was spinning tales—like always."

She shrugged. "Guess it can be hard to tell with Charlie."

Nick ran a hand through his hair, and Mitch chuckled again.

"So, did you know about me?" Nick asked.

"That is new to me," Jane admitted, and looked at Dom. "Scared the hell out of me, seeing a huge tiger running out of the woods."

He flinched again. "Sorry about that."

His voice was almost an octave deeper than normal, and the sound caressed along Jane's nerves like velvet. Damn, but that was bad. Why did she always get hot and bothered for the bad ones?

"You were in trouble," Dom went on. "I was only thinking about that."

His comment hit her right in her most vulnerable spot, that part of her that loved the idea of being so cared for by a man he'd do anything to keep her safe. She resented that part of herself, and yet the thought of Dom's protective instincts still made her giddy. She was such a fool.

"You're a pretty tiger," Ben said.

Dom raised his brows, and Jane had to press her lips together not to laugh at his expression.

"Your mom tell you to say that to me?" he asked Ben.

"Yes."

Dom met her gaze, the heat there making her stomach dance.

She looked away. "So what's the deal, then? There are werewolves in the world. Knew that already. You all are like that, only tigers?"

"About right," Dom said.

"Tiana said it wouldn't hurt the baby to shift. Does it hurt you?"

"No," Dom said. "It's natural to us. Just part of who we are."

"Do you…change humans to tigers, like werewolves do in the movies?"

"We can't." He glanced at Nick, then sighed. "Werewolves can change humans. It's not easy, though, and the local pack doesn't condone it."

"But you guys can't do it?"

"No."

"What else should I know?"

Dom shrugged. "What do you want to know?"

"How dangerous are you?"

"Dangerous as any tiger."

"You move a lot faster."

"We're faster. And stronger. We heal quickly."

"That's cool," Ben said. "How fast do you move?"

"Very," Jane said with feeling. "Gave me motion sickness."

"You got to do it?" Ben turned to look at her. "Can I?"

"We'll talk about that later." But not if she had any say in the matter. At least, not yet. Not until she could decide just how dangerous this tiger business was. She glanced at Nick and narrowed her eyes. "Is that why you all look so much younger than your ages?"

Dom's mouth ticked up. "Ben finally told you how old we are, huh?"

"Yes. And why didn't you tell me?"

"You never asked."

Her frown deepened. "Semantics. Is it the tiger thing? Or just good genes?"

"Both," Mitch said, waggling his eyebrows.

"Tigers age different than humans," Nick said. "So we tend to look younger than our biological age."

"How long do you live?"

"Depends."

"On what?"

"Lot of things."

Nick's gaze slid away as he said this and Jane frowned. She faced Dom. "On what things?" she asked.

"Whether we're killed in a fight. Get caught by a hunter. Break one of our laws and get put to death."

"Jesus, that happens?" She raised her brows. "What the hell kind of laws get you killed?"

"Killing humans is an automatic death sentence."

She blinked. "Well. That's a nice thing, then."

"Why?"

"Unless you're suicidal or crazy, you're not a big danger to the people here."

"We never were," Nick said.

"Yeah, well, I'm still adjusting so I'll decide about that later. Do most tigers follow these laws of yours?"

"They do," Dom said.

"How many of you are there?"

"Less than there used to be. We're on the brink of extinction. Not enough females. And…mostly, we can only have kids with other tigers."

She let the implications of that sink in for a few minutes. She looked at Mitch. "Your woman. She's a tiger?"

"She's…not," Mitch answered. "But her mother was."

"But you just said…"

"Turns out," Dom said, "some humans and tigers can mate. They make hybrids—some can shift into tigers, others are humans, like Mitch's fiancée."

"Hmm." Jane pursed her lips, letting all the information settle.

So…if she did give in to her attraction for Dom, and he didn't turn out to be a horrible choice—and her jury was still out on that point—then they weren't likely to have children together. She'd never planned on having any more anyway. She might not technically be too old, but she felt too old. Ben was all she needed by way of kids of her own. The idea that, even if she wanted more, they wouldn't be possible with the man she—

She cut herself off, not even close to ready for that line of thinking.

"So if nothing goes wrong," she said, "how long do you live?"

"Average?" Dom said. "About a hundred and twenty-five years or so. There are older tigers than that."

"How old's the oldest?"

The brothers exchanged a look, little half-smiles lightening Nick and Dom's serious expressions.

"We're pretty sure our grandmother is nearing a hundred and eighty or something like that," Dom said. "But she won't admit it."

"Jesus wept. That's some lifetime." Jane would have guessed Elizaveta was around seventy-five. She definitely assumed the woman was younger than Charlie Sanchez.

"Tigers have been known to live to two hundred," Mitch said.

"But like with long-lived humans," Dom said, "it's not common. The elders, our governing body, most of them are older than average."

"Well, that whole elder term kind of gives that fact away, doesn't it?" Jane said.

Dom's mouth lifted in another little smile. Her heartbeat thumped too hard and she cursed silently.

"Elder isn't necessarily a term of longevity so much as an honorific to mark their official office," Dom said. "But it takes influence, money, and a lot of cunning to get to be an elder, so the older tigers do tend to make the cut over younger ones."

"How many elders are there?" Ben asked.

His interest only mildly surprised Jane. He hadn't seemed like he was paying much attention. But it was always a mistake to assume Ben wasn't listening to every word spoken around him.

"There are eight now," Dom said, "but usually nine elders make up the official council."

"Why only eight?" Ben asked.

"One died. He hasn't been replaced yet."

Jane caught a subtle note in Dom's voice when he said died. There was more story there than he was saying aloud. But if he wasn't telling Ben everything, it was probably best not to push Dom for answers in front of her son. Likely, the truth was a little too scary. Ben had had more than enough of that for one night.

So had she. She glanced at the clock on the fireplace mantel. Three in the morning. She shook her head. She had the early shift at the diner.

As if reading her thoughts, Nick said, "Take tomorrow off. You've had a rough night."

"I'll be fine," she said.

"I'm your boss and what I say goes. You're taking tomorrow off. We can manage one day without you."

She snorted in mild disbelief, and Nick grinned.

Then he rose and motioned to his brothers. "If you're feeling better now, we'll leave you two to rest. Unless you want one of us to stay around, just in case?"

She hesitated. The thought of one of the werewolves coming back tonight did worry her. But she had her shotgun. Though she needed to go see Charlie's grandson Joe Sanchez tomorrow. She glanced at Ben, whose eyes were drooping.

"You think those thugs will come back?" she asked Nick.

"No," Dom answered. "Their leaders are taking care of them."

"You'll be safe now," Mitch added. "But I'll sleep on the couch if you want a guard cat."

He winked, and Jane chuckled.

Dom scowled at Mitch. Mitch raised his brows in an innocent look that was obviously an act. Dom grunted and nodded his brothers toward the front door.

"Go home and sleep," he told them. "I'll leave when Jane feels safe enough."

Mitch looked between Dom and Jane, his eyes narrowed. "Sure she's safe from you?"

"Out," Dom said.

"Goodnight, Mitch," Jane said at the same time.

Mitch grinned, unrepentant, slapped Nick on the shoulder and pushed him toward the front door.

Nick paused long enough to warn, "Don't show up at work tomorrow, Jane. I'll dock your pay if you do."

Then Nick and Mitch left. Closing the front door quietly behind them. Leaving Dom and Jane facing each other in silence.

"I'm going to sleep," Ben said, yawning around the comment. "You're safe with Dom."

She pulled Ben close for another hug, kissing him on the temple. "Thanks for helping me tonight, baby," she murmured. "You were so brave."

"I love you, Mom."

She smiled. "Love you, too. Sleep well."

She watched him amble out, stumbling a little with his exhaustion, and she got that familiar pang in her heart, her throat tightening with so much love she never knew quite what to do about it.

Pulling in a deep breath to ease some of the ache, she turned back to face Dom. He hadn't moved from his chair next to the couch, but somehow the space between them felt like it had closed in, like they were much nearer than they'd been just a moment ago. Without Ben as a buffer, Jane grew uncomfortably aware of the late-night silence, the intimacy of her cozy living room with the fire quietly crackling in the grate.

She swallowed hard, even as her pulse pounded louder in her ears. She needed to send Dom home. Having him here, when she was still feeling edgy and vulnerable, was a very bad idea. Even thoughts of the werewolf's disgusting looking change weren't enough to distract her from the look in Dom's eyes—heat, darkness, protective and possessive all at once. Her shoulders shook with a tremor that had nothing to do with cold.

"Should I stoke the fire?" he asked, his voice still deep and husky.

"It's fine."

He held her gaze, but she wasn't sure what she wanted to say to him. And so for a long moment, they just stared at each other, all the events of the last few hours hovering in the air around them.

"Were you ever going to tell me you could turn into a tiger?" she finally asked.

"Depended."

"On what?"

"On if you ever gave me a chance to be more to you than your boss' brother."

"If I didn't?"

"Then no. It's safer for you not to know about our world. We don't tell humans we exist, if we can help it."

"If I did give you a chance?"

"I would have told you. Eventually. Once I knew it wouldn't scare the hell out of you."

"Too late for that."

His shoulders dropped, and he let out a frustrated sigh. "Yeah."

"I'm not as scared as I should be."

"Good."

"Not good. Just another sign I'm terrible at picking men."

"Why?"

"You're a fucking tiger, Dom. You said yourself you're

dangerous. I saw what you and Mitch could do, the way you tossed those wolves around."

"They're lucky I knew their leaders were coming," he muttered.

"Why?"

"I would have torn them limb from limb for endangering you and Ben."

"You could have?"

"Easily."

She shivered and it wasn't from fear. Damn it. "Why do I always go for the wicked men?" she asked aloud, not really expecting an answer.

"I'm not a bad man, Jane. I'm protective. I won't apologize for that. And I won't apologize for wanting to hurt the men who might have seriously hurt you and Ben." He let out a breath and leaned forward, settling his forearms on his knees, holding her gaze. "Jane, I'm in love with you. I have been for years. The thought of anyone hurting you makes me want to do violence. I'm sorry if that scares you. But I can control that part of myself. And I would never turn it on you. You *have* to know that."

"You made sure Nick stayed with Ben tonight?"

"I did."

"You thought of Ben, even as you charged off to get me." She considered that, what that said about him.

"I'd protect you both with my life."

"Both of us?"

"Both of you."

"Well that says something, doesn't it?"

"I hope it says you can trust me."

"Still deciding on that." She made a face. "It's pretty sexy, though."

His mouth lifted at one corner, a half-smile that made her thighs clench.

"Stop that," she ordered.

"What?"

"Looking all hot and gorgeous. I need to think straight. You don't make that easy."

"I'm not really sorry about that either."

She snorted.

"You haven't commented on the fact that I just told you I love you."

"Yeah, well, I'm still processing that along with everything else."

"At least you're not running away."

"Yet," she warned.

"It gives me time to convince you I'm serious."

"I believe you're serious. I'm just not sure what to do about it."

"Consider it. Please."

He almost killed her with the "please." The "please" made it all the more sweet and sexy and…tempting.

"Can I…" He hesitated. "What happened tonight scared a few years off my life. Can I please hold you for just a few minutes? I won't push anything. I just…"

She lifted her chin, a bare nod of assent. She shouldn't agree to this, but she wanted to be held. More than she could admit to. She wanted Dom's big strong arms wrapped around her, an assurance she and Ben were safe. She'd be embarrassed about wanting reassurances from a man tomorrow. Tonight, she was just grateful he'd offered.

He settled next to her on the couch and she folded into him, clinging to his waist as he enveloped her in a tight hug. His heat and scent wound around her, warming the part of her still cold from fear and worry.

For a while, they sat in silence and she soaked up the feel of security. She didn't usually feel that way around men—somewhere in the back of her mind, even when she thought she was making sensible choices, she always knew she picked bad men and didn't ever feel completely safe with them.

Dom was different. She stared at the fire, feeling safer than she'd ever felt. Safer than she'd felt as a kid in her parents' overly protective home. She felt...at ease with Dom.

And then again not, because the hard feel of his muscles under her hands sent a lot of needy tingles through her stomach. It was way too easy to imagine pulling his too-tight t-shirt off and running her hands over his bare skin. Skin so hot it would scorch her. She snuggled closer, almost moaning when his arms tightened.

The mistakes of her past poked at the back of her mind, a nagging little voice that laughed at her lust and the sense of security she felt with Dom, laughed and taunted and reminded her it could only end badly.

For the first time in her life, she hated that voice. Hated it with a deep and abiding passion. Until now, that voice had had good reason to warn her away from the men she wanted. To remind her how bad she was at choosing men.

But with Dom, that voice sounded…false. Like a liar. Dom felt right, and good.

Oh, but she'd thought that before, hadn't she? With Grace's husband? With the trucker, before he'd told her to abandon her "retarded" son? Didn't she always convince herself the warning voice of her conscience was wrong *this time*?

"You're thinking too hard," Dom commented.

She snorted. "How'd you know?"

"I could practically hear it."

"I want to believe you're different."

"Good."

"But I've talked myself into believing that before. And that's a problem. Because I was always wrong to believe a man was different."

"Were any of them tiger shifters?"

"Well… No. Not that I know of."

"There you go, then."

"Huh?" She lifted up enough to look him in the face."

"I am different. Extremely different from anyone else you've ever known."

She stared at him before a chuckle took her. She shook her head and settled back against his side. "Can't argue with that."

"Your voice is scratchy from being tired," he said. "Sleep. You'll feel better in the morning."

"Maybe." She'd feel better if she could trust her own damned heart. Because her heart wanted to take Dom up to her bed and spend the hours until sunrise exploring every inch of him.

She hadn't been with a man in a very long time, not since coming to Eirene eight years ago. She had a lot of pent-up lust, and Dom was exactly the person she wanted to release all that lust on.

He was stroking her arm, his fingers caressing over her shoulder, almost absently, unconsciously. The sensation set her nerves alight, tingling with awareness. There was always so much *awareness* around Dom—of her own body, the way her skin felt tighter, and hotter, whenever he was close. Awareness of his body, those strong shoulders and thick arms that made her mouth water… At least she knew how he stayed so fit now. Probably came naturally to a man who could turn into a tiger, even if his job kept him in front of a computer.

"You're still thinking too much," he said.

"Yeah, well, you'd probably approve of what I'm thinking about now."

"If you tell me, will it make me forget I promised not to push anything?"

"Probably."

"Then you shouldn't tell me what you're thinking."

"No. I shouldn't." She was silent for a moment. "I was thinking how much I love your body. How much I'd really like to strip off that shirt and finally get my hands on what's underneath."

His fingers stopped moving, but his arm muscles bunched. So did his stomach muscles under her hand. Every part of him she was touching tensed and got harder. And because she wasn't looking him in the face, she savored that sensation. The girly part of herself she usually ignored was more than a little thrilled with the way he reacted to her.

"Jane…" His voice was hoarse and deep, guttural.

The sound made her toes curl.

"Tigers…" He paused and she heard him swallow. "Tigers have a very good sense of smell."

"Meaning."

"I can…tell what you're feeling right now, from your scent."

She nodded, her heart thumping so painfully hard in her chest she thought he might be able to feel it.

"I'm trying very hard not to take advantage of the fact that you've had a scary night and are looking for comfort," he said. "But Jane, your scent is driving me crazy. All I can think about is tasting you."

"That comment should scare me since you turn into a tiger occasionally."

"If you were scared, I'd have an easier time controlling myself right now."

"Yeah, I'm not even a little scared of the idea of you tasting me."

He groaned and his hand flexed on her arm. "You're killing me."

She laughed, but it was strained. "Not doing myself any favors, either."

She couldn't resist a glance down. Through the too-tight sweat pants, his erection was obvious. And solid. And oh did she want to run her hands down to the straining ridge of his cock and…play.

"Should I leave?" he said, his voice so deep now it was little more than a growl.

Her fingers twitched against his stomach, and she did move her hand a little lower, marveling at how wonderful it felt when his body tensed even tighter at her touch. "You probably should leave," she murmured. "But I'm not going to let you."

"Thank god."

He lifted her chin, turning her unresisting mouth up to his for a kiss that burned her from the inside out. She surprised herself with how easy it was to fall into that kiss, to take his mouth with all her pent-up hunger and not regret it even a little bit. She let the blanket fall from her shoulders and crawled around to straddle his lap, settling her heat tight against his hard cock, swallowing his groan. He gripped her hips, his fingers hard but restrained.

She didn't want restrained. Now that she'd opened the door and released her lust, she didn't want him holding back either.

"Harder," she grunted. "Rough. Don't try to be gentle."

His arms came around her, tight and hard, pulling her against his chest. Her breasts flattened against his muscles and for the first time in years she felt lush and feminine and…free. She rubbed against him, loving the way the friction made her nipples hard, loving the way his cock jumped against her.

They didn't have a lot of clothing between them, but what they did have was too much. She ran her hands down his arms, up again and into his hair, holding his head close for a long, deep kiss. He tasted so damned good it made her head spin. She licked her way down his throat, nipping his shoulder through his shirt, chuckling when he growled. He dropped his hands to her ass and squeezed tight, not holding back now, and she arched into this grip, loving his rough touch.

"Upstairs?" he asked, the sound of his voice muted against her neck as he nibbled his way over her throat, to her collarbone.

"God, yes."

"The fire will be okay?"

She glanced back, a little too dazed to think about reality, but forcing herself to take in the low flames. "Safe enough with the grate in front of it. It's dying down."

"Good, because I'm not sure I have enough control to stop and put the fire out."

She chuckled, loving the way her breasts rubbed against him when she did. He responded to the sensation by tightening his hold on her ass. She started to back off his lap, but he didn't let her. Instead, with a strength that made her gasp, he simply stood up holding her as if she weighed nothing, and turned toward the stairs.

"You're very strong," she commented, her voice breathy and choked from all the desire rolling through her.

"You can't even imagine how hard it was for me to let Mitch carry you earlier."

She ducked her head, unnecessarily, as he stalked up the stairs. "I like having you carry me more, if that helps." She spoke quietly now, because Ben's room was up here and even if he was a sound sleeper, she didn't want to risk waking him. She wasn't sure how she'd explain this to him.

She realized in a brief flash of reality that this was the first time she'd let a man into her bed, in her own home, with Ben around. She usually kept her sex life well separate from her son, when she'd had a sex life.

The thought was almost enough to poke a hole in her lust-induced daze. But then Dom kissed her again and any kind of logic scrambled and fled under the hard demand of his lips on hers.

He pushed into her room—she didn't even have to direct him; should that worry her?—and then quietly he closed the door behind him, turning the lock.

She smiled against his mouth before sinking back into his kiss.

Her bedroom was pitch black. She wasn't sure he'd find the bed without them both falling, but she couldn't lift away from the taste of him long enough to comment on it. And before she knew it, he had her sprawled on the mattress, as if finding the bed was easy and natural.

She had his shirt off fast, because she'd wanted her hands on his bare skin for so long it was almost beyond her control to resist any longer. He was so hard, so hot, so damned solid. She traced the muscles over his chest, scraped her nails over his nipples, purred when he groaned and bit her lower lip gently—but not too gently.

His weight over her was maybe the best thing she'd ever felt in her entire life. Rivaled only by the feel of his hard cock pressed against her thigh. He stripped off her flannel and t-shirt, removed her bra without her realizing he had, and then his lips closed over her straining nipple. She had to bite her own lip to keep from screaming.

Her body strained toward him, writhed beneath him, and even without his hands going anywhere near her clit, she wanted to come.

She got tighter and hotter and wetter when he moved down her stomach, his tongue a lapping instrument of torture she couldn't get enough of. His hands were rough, jerking her jeans open and down her hips without any pretense at civility. God, she loved it.

She heard her underwear rip. She loved that, too. And then his mouth was on her, licking across her and into her and doing things to her that hadn't been done in much too long, and she couldn't hold anything back. She had enough sense in her head to bite down on a pillow so she didn't really scream, but that was as much as she could manage. He licked, he sucked, he nibbled, and she came so hard her entire body felt like it disintegrated in one blinding flash of pleasure.

He didn't let her recover. Her body still trembling from the orgasm, he set his fingers and mouth to sending her up again. Pleasure and heat and the building tension wrapping her up in so much sensation she forgot her own damned name. Then she was coming again, hard and sharp, and she did scream this time, her voice muffled in the pillow.

She collapsed, her face still half-buried under the pillow, and panted, trying to force her rubbery arms to move. She wanted to touch him, taste him, but in that moment, she only had enough energy to breathe.

When he rose over her, settling between her legs, she pushed the pillow away so she could look at him. He looked a little smug and a lot sexy. God, so sexy. She pulled him down for a kiss, surprising herself with the strength of her need for him. Six years of wanting, six years of telling herself she'd *never* allow this, had left her a lot more on edge than she'd guessed and way too vulnerable.

He kissed her deeply, but when she felt his cock nudge against her entrance, she pulled back. "Condom?"

"I can't get you pregnant."

"Diseases?"

He grinned. "We can't spread those to humans either."

"You're like some kind of fantasy dream."

His expression turned serious. "You're my fantasy."

He kissed her again, lingering but not soft and gentle. Deep and heady and full of everything he'd said earlier and everything still left to be said between them. She welcomed him, wrapping her legs around his hips as he slid into her, the stretch of him taking her breath. He wasn't a small man, in any sense of the word, and she'd been celibate for years. But her body was so primed and ready for him, the friction felt delicious, perfect. And while his entrance was torturously slow, he didn't set a slow pace.

After only a moment of getting each other's rhythm, he fucked her hard, and rough, just the way she wanted him to. His mouth on her breast, his fingers digging into her thighs, his hips slamming down as she slammed up, the sounds of their bodies coming together filling the room, matched only by the sounds of their moans and grunts.

Sweat dripped down her temples as she raced with him, her hands rough on his shoulders and back, scraping her nails over his skin, digging her fingers into his tight ass as he pumped into her. She bit his lip, he sucked her earlobe, she told him how good he felt, he cursed. She took every single bit of strength and passion he gave her greedily, self-ishly, because she'd wanted this for too long and there was no more holding back.

The third orgasm took her by surprise and she bit his shoulder hard to keep quiet as her body jerked against his. He cursed again, buried his face against her neck and followed her, groaning her name as he came with a sharp, slamming jerk of his hips.

Jane blinked the sweat out of her eyes when Dom rose to look down at her. He cupped her face in one hand, kissed her gently, and Jane felt her world rearranging itself as Dom filled in the gaps in her life she hadn't even known were there.

CHAPTER EIGHT

Boneless and happy and scared all at once, Jane snuggled close to Dom. What had she done? And what disaster would come from this?

Except it didn't feel like a disaster. She felt amazing. And settled. And better than she had in a very long time.

"Don't start thinking yet," Dom said, his arm tight around her, his eyes closed. He'd rolled onto his back, but he'd kept her firmly pressed against his side.

She grinned because he couldn't see her. "Why not?"

"Cause I can't think enough yet to argue with you."

She chuckled. "Fine. I'll try not to think. Given that's the first sex I've had in more than eight years, I'm too tired to think anyway."

"More than eight years, huh?"

"I gave up men when I moved to Eirene."

"How did you go that long without an orgasm?"

She raised her brows. "I didn't. I know how to pump my own gas."

He cracked his eyes open to look at her. And she almost laughed at his expression.

"I'm not sure whether to be turned on at the thought, or appalled that you went all that time 'pumping your own gas' when I would have been overjoyed to help."

"You did. Who do you think I was fantasizing about?"

He groaned. "That doesn't make me feel better."

Grinning, she gave him a brief kiss. "Tell you what, you can help in person now. For a little while anyway."

"Deal. Except for that 'a little while' part."

"Meaning?"

"Meaning I want more than just a little while. But I'll take what I can get now."

"What you got was pretty damned good."

"Absolutely." He closed his eyes again and hugged her close. "I knew it would be. Which is why I want more."

She hesitated because she wasn't supposed to be thinking and because she didn't want to break the mood. It had been a very long time since she'd been this content in bed with a man. But still, it was only fair to be honest with him.

"I'm not sure how much more I can give, Dom."

"I'm patient. The past six years have proven that already."

He grumbled that last, and she chuckled.

"I can wait for you to trust me," he said. "But I intend to give you lots of orgasms in the meantime."

"Well, that I can take."

"Good. Now sleep. That'll put off all this thinking business for a few more hours. And you've had a busy night."

"Damn straight. Glad your brother made me take the day off."

"Me, too. Sleep."

"You staying until I wake up?"

"So long as you don't mind. Ben will know if I do. Are you okay with that?"

She considered how she felt about Ben knowing she'd spent the night with Dom. She'd been so meticulous over the years, keeping her love life and Ben separate. All of that went out the window with Dom. But then, Ben was the one who'd told them to kiss and get married.

"He is eighteen now," she said aloud. Then, "Jesus, my baby is eighteen. When the hell did that happen? Where did the time go?"

Dom hugged her a little tighter. "He's a good man, Jane. You've done a good job raising him."

Snuggling her head under Dom's chin, she sighed. "Thanks. Wasn't always easy. But worth it."

"You think he'll approve of the fact that I finally kissed you?"

"Think he'd be nagging us both if you hadn't."

Dom laughed quietly. "Then I'll stay. If it upsets him, we'll change things around. Last thing I want is to upset him."

If she hadn't already been in deep with Dom, she'd have probably been more surprised when the ground gave out beneath her in that moment, tumbling her head over heels into emotions she'd been denying for years.

Love. Wasn't that the end all?

Jane woke late the next morning to an empty bed and conflicting emotions. Anger because he'd said he'd stay. Relief because now she didn't have to explain Dom staying the night to Ben.

She still wasn't sure how to explain it to herself. Six years of resistance had crumbled and left her vulnerable. She hated being vulnerable. She'd been there too often in the past and now it just pissed her off.

But…

But, she had to admit, last night had been the best, most mind-blowing night of sex she'd ever had. There was more to it than the sex, she'd admit that, too—in private if not out loud. She wanted more of what they'd shared. Days, weeks, months of it. Years.

She pressed her hand to her forehead and stared up at her bedroom ceiling. Silly, silly woman. She was going to get hurt. And once again, she'd run right into trouble with a big fat fucking smile.

She rolled out of bed and took a quick shower before heading downstairs. Ben would have been up for hours, and he could make his own breakfast, but if he hadn't eaten more than potato chips and milk, she'd make him something.

As she came down the stairs, the sound of her son's voice from the kitchen made her smile. The sound of a deeper, older voice talking with him made her pause.

Dom was agreeing with something Ben said, and Ben

went on a ramble about…she was pretty sure it was the latest game he was testing. He really liked the one he'd started last night before her kidnapping. Sounded like he was telling Dom all about it.

Her heart clenched tight when she heard Dom's quiet but real interest in what her son had to say. She closed her eyes, trying to settle her emotions. Failed miserably. Then headed to the kitchen to say good morning to the two men in her life.

Dom looked up and caught her gaze the instant she stepped into the room. His smile was soft and questioning, as if he wasn't sure of her mood.

Since she wasn't sure of it either, she decided he was a wise man. Looking at him, standing all sexy and big and relaxed in her kitchen, made her heart pound hard, a tingling of excitement and lust settling in her gut. It was entirely too easy, imagining him there every morning.

She shook off the fear and longing to take in the scene. Then she raised her brows. Ben stood at the toaster, buttering two well-done slices of bread. Dom stood over the stove stirring a pan full of scrambled eggs. The microwave dinged and Ben went to pull out a plate of bacon covered by paper towels. The scent of crispy bacon filled the kitchen and made her mouth water.

Ben smiled over his shoulder at her. "Good morning."

"Morning. You two making yourselves breakfast?"

"This is for you," Ben said.

"His idea," Dom added.

"You guys made *me* breakfast?" Another tight little

clench of her heart. "That was very sweet. What's the occasion?"

"Ben thought you'd be hungry after last night," Dom said.

She almost gasped aloud. Glaring at Dom, she said, "What about last night would make him think that?"

"You got kidnapped," Ben said, his back to her as he patted the bacon with the paper towel. "I'd be hungry after that. Cause it's cold. The cold always makes me hungry."

Her shoulders relaxed and she huffed out a half-embarrassed grunt when Dom gave her a raised-eyebrow look. Smart ass.

"Go sit down at the table," Ben said, missing the silent exchange between Jane and Dom. "I'll bring your plate."

Her son making her breakfast was enough of a distraction—and a surprise—to get her past her mild discomfort at having Dom there. "When did you learn to make bacon?" she asked Ben.

"Emma taught me. She likes bacon."

It was on the tip of her tongue to ask more questions about Emma and bacon and exactly when and where they were eating bacon, but she realized she didn't want to have that conversation in front of Dom. Instead, she sat at the small table that took up the open half of her kitchen and watched Dom help Ben get the eggs on a plate. They'd made enough to feed a small army, she noticed. But when Dom put food on two more plates, she wondered if it was enough—she'd seen how much Dom could eat.

She finally understood how he could eat so much and stay in shape.

The whole tiger shifter thing had gotten shoved to the back of her mind last night. Now, the reminder started her thinking again, worrying. She was good at worrying.

She wasn't sure what worried her more, though. That she was in love with a man who'd likely break her heart. Or that the man she loved occasionally turned into a tiger.

Sitting around her kitchen table with Ben and Dom felt entirely too comfortable and easy. Ben and Dom talked about games almost non-stop and Dom was so involved Jane couldn't help but smile. He wasn't just tolerating Ben's current subject of choice. He was actively discussing Ben's passion with him.

Their breakfast proved to be delicious—and needed. She hadn't even realized how hungry she was until she took her first bite of bacon. Ben preened, in his shy way, when she complimented his cooking skills, and then he went back to rambling about video games and apps.

The meal was the kind of thing she'd wanted so badly as a younger woman, the type of family scene she hadn't allowed herself to want in years. And the fact that Dom fit into her and Ben's family dynamic so easily scared the ever-loving crap out of her.

When the dishes were finished and Ben had gone back to his tablet and another app game, Dom caught her for a secretive kiss at the kitchen door. The feel of his arms around her, his mouth against hers, brought back all the wonderful release of the night before and she almost forgot herself, leaning into him for more.

"I can't even tell you how happy I am that I can finally kiss you with abandon," he murmured.

"I'd still rather we didn't kiss too much in front of Ben," she said, easing back but keeping her arms around his neck.

"That's the only reason I waited this long to kiss you good morning. Did you sleep well?"

"Best I've slept in years," she said in absolute honesty.

"Good. Me too."

She grinned, the fluttering in her chest at his smile something she'd worry about later.

"I need to head back to the motel," he said. "To shower and change. Then I need to talk to Nick about what happened last night."

She raised her brows, and he snorted.

"You know what I mean. The wolves."

"I know. But your brother is going to ask about us."

"It's none of his business."

"He's still my boss."

"Who won't put his nose where it doesn't belong."

Well, that was probably true enough. The good thing about Eirene, even though it was a small town, and everyone was curious about what was happening with everyone else, no one got into anyone else's business uninvited. Most of the time.

"Can I see you later?" Dom asked. "Dinner?"

"Like a date? I haven't been on one of those in years."

"A date. Dinner out—not at the diner even if the food is excellent and it would be fun to watch Nick cook for us."

"Not at the diner," she agreed.

"Vail?"

She pursed her lips, thinking about Ben—old enough to

be on his own at college but somehow she still felt guilty leaving him alone in the evening for too long. Old habits.

"Bet Tiana and Nick would love to have Ben visit," Dom said into her silence.

She laughed. "How did you know what I was thinking about?"

"I know you."

"That scares the hell out of me."

"I know that, too." He kissed her again, a gentle brush of lips. "I'll call later this afternoon to set a time. Enjoy your day off."

She closed the front door behind him, frowning because Tiana had brought him a sweatshirt and shoes last night, but he didn't have a coat and it was still freezing outside. The fact that she was worrying over a man who could turn into a tiger at will was more than a little ridiculous.

And only proved how deeply in trouble she was.

* * *

Dom returned to his truck parked in front of Nick's house and drove back to the motel without stopping to say anything to his brother or sister-in-law. He wasn't ready to talk about what had happened between him and Jane yet, a part of him afraid if he did, he would somehow jinx everything. He'd never considered himself particularly superstitious, but with Jane, he was afraid to take anything for granted.

On the drive back to his motel, a little outside of town, close to the highway, but the only one in the area, he considered his business and the work he'd been doing for Victor at the elders' compound. Moving to Eirene wouldn't be any trouble for Dom—so long as Nick was okay with it since this was Nick's territory. Dom loved the town and felt more comfortable here than in his own house in Vermont. But he and Victor weren't done revamping the security at the compound yet. And when he was done with that, he'd have to move some things around so he could run his business from Eirene.

He should look into getting a house here, too. He was sure Jane was nowhere near ready to move in with him, and while the three-story motel he was staying in was quaint and comfortable, he didn't like living out of motel rooms the way Mitch did. So he'd need a place of his own. He had a lot to discuss with his brother.

He was barely through the door of his first-floor room when his cellphone rang. Nick's number. "What's up?" he asked as he started undressing for a shower.

"You left without stopping to say hi."

"Had some thinking to do. Why aren't you at work?"

"I am. How's Jane this morning?"

"Good."

"Good good or just okay?"

Dom scowled at the wall. "Meaning?"

"Meaning, have you two finally…settled things. And if so, is that something to celebrate or should I be sending sympathies and beer to the motel?"

Dom snorted and sat on the edge of the bed to pull off his borrowed running shoes. "No need for beer and sympathy. At the moment. I do need to talk to you about moving to Eirene."

"Tiana will be thrilled."

"How about you?"

"No other tiger I'd rather have living in town with us. Except maybe Mitch."

Dom chuckled. "Thanks, Nick. It'll take some time to transition."

"Will Victor let you go? I know he doesn't trust anyone else to help him at the moment."

"That'll be part of the transition."

"How does Jane feel about you moving here? Or are you moving in with her?"

"I haven't even mentioned it to her yet. And don't you spill the beans early," he warned. "But I figure we'll have an easier time if I'm close enough that she can't ignore me."

Nick barked a laugh. "Right. Easier. Because Jane is so easy to deal with."

Dom rolled his eyes at his brother's sarcasm.

Nick paused, then said, "Hold on a sec."

The phone was muffled but Dom still heard Nick talking to someone—sounded like the waitress covering for Jane that morning.

Then Nick was back. "I need to go, the grill is calling, but come by the diner when you're ready. We have things to talk about."

"Be there in an hour." He frowned a little. "Elizaveta arrives day after tomorrow, right?"

"Right. Why? You worried grandma won't approve? You know she will. She likes Jane."

"I just don't want her…getting involved. Things are still delicate between me and Jane. And you know how Elizaveta is."

Nick groaned. "I understand. Don't even get Mitch started on that topic."

Dom grinned. "I just want a chance to talk more with Jane before she's exposed to our grandmother's machinations."

"You sure she hasn't been already?"

Dom closed his eyes. "You just scared the hell out of me. Get back to work. See you in an hour."

Dom stared at the wall for a long moment after he disconnected with Nick. Jane had met the various members of his family before. They all liked her. There was no reason to worry about them screwing things up. Obviously, Nick and Tiana approved. Mitch would tease, but he wouldn't do anything to fuck things up for Dom. Alexis and Jane got along well…

Elizaveta was the real wildcard. His grandmother had *ideas* about the way things were supposed to happen, and she was frighteningly good at manipulating situations and people. She knew how he felt about Jane because she'd met Jane while Dom was around. Dom couldn't hide the emotions that roared through his scent whenever Jane was nearby, not from his grandmother.

But she'd never said anything, one way or the other. She'd never even hinted at approval or disapproval. That lack of information from Elizaveta was unnerving. And worrying. Despite what Nick said, if their grandmother wanted to, she would have no qualms about trying to scare Jane off—because she was human; because she couldn't give Dom children; because her son was autistic and any kind of perceived mental disability was an issue among the tigers…

But Elizaveta had welcomed Victor into the family with open arms—even though many tigers considered his inability to talk a mental flaw rather than a physical one. And Elizaveta's own son—and grandsons for that matter—had suffered under the tiger intolerance for mental flaws. She had to be sympathetic.

Dom pulled off the rest of his borrowed clothes and climbed into the shower, a space actually big enough to accommodate him. He didn't consider Ben's autism a "mental disability" the way other tigers might. It was just part of who Ben was and Ben was fantastic. But the way Dom felt about it wasn't common among his people. He already had a huge stigma on his name, just by being a Chernikov who'd come from a mother who'd committed suicide and a father who'd had a mental breakdown.

Until that moment, Dom hadn't thought about how complicated it might be to bring Jane into his world because of Ben. Frankly, he'd been afraid to think about it, worried that even considering it might somehow drive Jane farther away.

He had to think about it now. He couldn't give her up, but he needed her and Ben safe. And he'd do whatever it took to do that, including staying in Eirene, cut off from most of the tiger world.

Only in Eirene, while Dom could avoid the other tigers, they still had a werewolf pack to contend with. If Gabriel couldn't get his pack in order, or disapproved of yet another tiger moving in next door, there *would* be trouble. Would Dom be helping the town or making things worse by settling here?

He scrubbed his hair and worried.

And wished he had Jane here so he could stop worrying and just hold her again. Pretending the rest of the world didn't exist and wouldn't interfere with their future.

CHAPTER NINE

Dom wandered into Nick's diner during the lull between the lunch and dinner rushes. The waitress on duty, Beth Anne, grinned at him and motioned him to the counter seats.

"Hey, Dom."

Her eyes twinkled in a way that made him frown. Beth Anne was in her early twenties, in a steady relationship with Charlie Sanchez's great grandson, according to Tiana, and one of Jane's neighbors. The smirking grin Beth Anne was giving Dom didn't bode well for his and Jane's night together having gone unnoticed.

Well, it was a small town after all. And he was about to become a regular resident. His relationship with Jane wouldn't be secret from everyone for much longer.

"You want some coffee? Anything to eat?" Beth Anne asked, wiping down the counter in front of him.

"I can always eat. Nick in the kitchen?"

"He is. I'll tell him to surprise you. He's been working on a few things." She winked and wandered back to the kitchen instead of putting an order through the window.

Charlie Sanchez, in his usual seat at the edge of the counter, gave Dom a nod topped off by a gummy, smug-looking grin.

Dom snorted a half-laugh and nodded to Charlie. He'd have to get used to small-town living. Eirene was unique as far as small towns went, at least in Dom's experience. The townsfolk were good at letting a person keep their secrets. No one dug into your past if you wanted to keep it quiet. And no one pushed for more than you were willing to give. But that didn't mean they didn't notice everything everyone did.

Hell, apparently, they all knew about werewolves. Dom had a feeling the people of Eirene would take just about anything with an easy acceptance. Jane had told him once that she thought of this place as the Island of Misfit Toys from an old Christmas cartoon. He'd always liked that description.

He liked it even better now that he was going to make this town his home.

Nick came out of the kitchen a few minutes later, carrying a plate piled high with food—beef roast covered in a rich looking sauce, potatoes, cooked winter vegetables and a bowl of something…black. Dom frowned at the bowl when Nick put it in front of him.

"I'm experimenting with squid-ink pasta again," Nick said. "Trust me, this is tasty."

"Which is why you also brought me a plate of meat and potatoes?" Dom said with a smirk.

"A bribe to get you to try the pasta."

Dom chuckled and dug in. He wasn't actually surprised that the pasta dish was delicious, with a strong briny fish taste that came as much from the sauce as the black pasta. Nick was a superb cook. But he could see why Nick had trouble getting a dish of black pasta past most of the diner's patrons.

"Good," Dom grunted.

Nick grinned as Dom moved on to the meat and potatoes after cleaning the pasta bowl.

"Finally! Someone with good taste."

"Does Tiana like your experiments?"

"Yes. And not just with food."

Dom raised a hand. "Don't say anything more. I don't want to know."

Nick laughed again. But his smile fell away and a furrow formed between his brows, his gaze shifting to the diner's front windows.

"What's wrong?" Dom asked, glancing over his shoulder briefly but not seeing anything.

"How did you know?"

"Years of practice. Is this about me moving here?"

From the kitchen, Beth Anne squealed.

Nick rolled his eyes. "Now you've done it. You better talk to Jane soon. I'm not the one who'll spill the beans early." He nodded over his shoulder.

Dom sighed. "I'll go see her after we talk." He could hardly wait to see her anyway. He was supposed to be calling, to set a time for their date. But a phone call wasn't enough for Dom. He wanted a pre-date kiss if Jane would let him steal one—and maybe more if Ben wasn't home.

"But it wasn't you moving here that had me frowning," Nick said. "I just saw Adam Walsh's car roll by."

Dom went onto immediate alert. He liked the pack beta, but he didn't trust any of the wolves at the moment. What had happened last night…that went way beyond the pale, especially inside Nick's territory. The tension that had dissipated at the meeting between Nick and the alpha the night before had ratcheted up again after Jane's kidnapping. And only because this was Nick's territory, and Dom wanted to move into it, did Dom keep his seat and not go looking for the pack beta. He wanted answers and consequences. If the werewolf leaders hadn't done enough to punish the bastards who'd endangered Jane and Ben, Dom would go hunting, and would ensure punishment himself.

He didn't doubt his brothers would hunt with him.

"Adam will be here as soon as he finds parking," Nick said. "Might want to finish up that meal. This could get…interesting."

"He'll come here?" Dom asked. "He's not just in town to see his sister?"

"After last night?" Nick said, so quietly only Dom would hear. "He's here to talk."

Dom shoveled down the rest of his meal as they waited.

* * *

J ane puttered around the house, cleaning and doing laundry and mainly trying to keep busy so she didn't think too much. Not that it helped. She still spent entirely too much time thinking. And whenever Ben wasn't in the room, she'd find herself remembering—in entirely too much detail—her night with Dom. Making her bed had only made things worse since Dom's smell was all over her sheets and pillows now. God, the man smelled good.

She kept herself busy until mid-afternoon, then gave in to her restlessness. "I'm going to see Joe Sanchez," she told Ben. "You need anything while I'm out?"

"Nope. Think Nick will make me a pizza for dinner?"

She smiled and shook her head because Ben was staring at his tablet and couldn't see her face. Nick had made the mistake of letting Ben make special requests for food. Now Ben thought Nick was his personal chef—especially for pizza. She had to admit, Nick did make a mean pizza.

"If you ask nicely, I'm sure he will. Be sure to bring the leftovers home for breakfast. I'll be back in an hour." She kissed him on the top of the head. He patted her hand but didn't look up from his game.

She grabbed her coat, purse and keys, but before she opened the front door, Ben called to her.

"Be careful, Mom."

Even though she couldn't see him, she heard the tremble in his voice, and it broke her heart. "I will, baby. You be careful, too. Keep your phone handy and text me if you need me."

"'Kay."

She locked the door behind her, angrier than she cared to show Ben at the fact that he was scared for her now. It wasn't his job to worry about her. It was her job to worry about him. That was the natural order to things.

She didn't bother with her car since Joe's pharmacy was along Main Street. It was easier to just walk than find parking close by this time of year, especially with a fresh snow and the street plow pushing all that extra snow up against the sidewalks. She mostly walked to and from work as well—one of the many things she loved about where she lived.

She turned onto Main Street, heading in the opposite direction of Nick's diner, her hands stuffed into her coat pocket, the clean cold air making puffs of smoke out of her breath. The holiday lights in the trees were already on, soft bright spots that would come to glowing life in a few more hours along with the snowflake decorations strung over the street. The mid-winter daylight was fading to darkness fast, filling the air with that strange twilight dimness that was harder to see in than full dark. The shop windows were bright and homey in contrast to the gray skies.

Jane pulled in a deep, cold breath and let it out slowly, savoring the feel of her beloved town. She pushed into the pharmacy a lot less angry than she'd been just fifteen minutes earlier—though no less determined.

"Hey, Jane." Joe waved from behind the pharmacy counter and came around to meet her. "Hear you had an interesting night."

"Oh?"

"You and Dom finally…" He winked. Jane scowled. He had the grace to blush.

"None of your business, Joe Sanchez. I'm here to talk about those things your grandfather taught you to make. I need a box." She didn't want to risk scaring the tourists, so she kept her voice quiet and her request vague on purpose.

His eyebrows jumped up. "I thought everything with *them* was settled, thanks to Nick."

"Well, there's some trouble. And I need a box. Good for my shotgun. You got something that'll work?"

"You sure you need that many? I gotta charge you for them. They're expensive to make. Silver doesn't grow on trees."

"A whole box," she said firmly. "And you might want to make up some extras. Just in case."

"You think we're gonna have the same kind of trouble we did before?" Joe asked quietly, all seriousness now.

"Not sure. Not taking any chances after that confrontation Nick had with those two thugs yesterday." She didn't want to scare the town by letting them know about her kidnapping. That had really been between the wolves and the Chernikovs more than the people of Eirene. But trouble had come into her house and scared her son. That wasn't going to happen again.

Joe nodded. "Siobhan Walsh *has* been having some visitors lately," he said, acknowledging what they all knew —Siobhan was a werewolf and her "visitors" were the wolves that had harassed the town before.

They all liked Siobhan and her shop well enough. None of them liked the trouble her "relatives" could cause.

"Let me go check what I've got here," Joe said. "I'll be right back."

Jane hovered near the back of the pharmacy as she waited, nodding hello to people she knew. The Sanchez family had been making silver bullets for generations, but for the last thirty years or so, the precaution hadn't been necessary so their stock had dwindled down to nearly nothing. After the last bout of trouble they'd had with the wolf pack, Joe Sanchez had started producing more, stocking up again. Just in case. No one wanted to make Nick completely responsible for their safety. It wasn't fair to him. He'd done enough, helping them when they weren't at the ready to help themselves. Now, everyone was prepared. Most people in town with a gun had at least two silver bullets in the house. The sheriff and deputies had several boxes in different calibers, so Jane understood.

Jane asking for a whole box was gonna start a Christmas run on the things. She doubted Joe would complain about the extra income. But none of them wanted to have to use that particular ammunition.

Joe came back out with a paper bag wrapped around a box. "There's only about ten in here," he said. "I'll get you some more in the next couple of days. I'll have to make them."

"When you can," Jane said. "This'll be enough for now. Thanks. What do I owe you?"

They settled the tab and Jane left feeling significantly more prepared for the damned wolves now. Let them come back to her home again. She'd teach them to mess with a protective momma.

* * *

Adam Walsh walked into the diner like any other customer, but his shoulders and scent were full of his tension. He nodded a greeting to Dom and made a hand gesture to Nick, silently asking where he should sit.

Dom didn't hesitate to join the conversation. After all, Adam's pack had endangered Dom's mate. That meant something in their world. And it put Dom square in the middle of this situation.

In a wolf show of contrition, Adam kept his gaze averted from Nick's as they settled in a booth near one of the diner's front windows.

"How's the woman?" Adam asked quietly, keeping his voice at a level that would be almost impossible for any of the surrounding humans to hear.

"Jane Emmerson," Nick said. "She's my head waitress."

"And my mate," Dom added.

"I figured that last part out," Adam said, without cracking a smile. "Frank only targeted her because of her relationship with you."

That didn't make Dom feel any better about the situation. But he wasn't going to take the blame either. "Is he dead?"

Adam blinked, and Dom frowned. The wolf's scent was full of things Dom couldn't quite read, but Dom's comment had brought up a hesitance in the beta's body language.

"No," Adam said slowly. "Gabriel decreed something that in the wolf world is considered much worse."

"But we're not going to like it, are we?" Nick asked.

"Depends. Frank has been banished from the pack. No other pack will take him now. He's…ostracized, outcast."

"Yeah, I don't like it," Dom said. "He threatened a human's life, and her son. Out of spite and maliciousness. Just to call me out for a fight. That put your entire pack in danger. He should be killed."

"He would have been if he'd been a tiger," Nick added. "Or at least locked up for years."

Neither Nick nor Dom brought up their father, but it hung in the air between them. Their father had been locked up for killing a human—a man who'd been beating a woman who bore a very vague resemblance to their mother. In the tiger world, that usually brought an automatic death sentence, especially because their father had killed the man in tiger form.

The only thing that had saved his life was the fact that his mother was an elder. She'd paid a lot of money for leniency, sacrificed a lot by way of her grandsons' status in the community, and the killing had happened before human forensics had really taken off.

These days, their father would never have survived his crimes. As it was, once he was out of confinement, he'd started stalking another human woman who looked vaguely like his lost mate. He went back to confinement, and once he was out, left the country. None of them had seen their father in years. Mostly, they'd been glad of it.

"You have to understand," Adam said, "with wolves the pack is everything. Without a pack, a lone wolf is…not just vulnerable…" He raised his hands in a kind of helpless shrug. "It's hard to explain if you're not a wolf because it's instinctive, part of our very makeup. We *need* to belong to a pack. Lone wolves suffer mentally if they remain outside pack structure for too long. They also become targets of other packs, so they're constantly on the move. They can't rest. They feel a constant state of edginess and fear. A fear they can't really control or master. Their brains won't let them. Even strong wolves end up going insane."

"Isn't that dangerous? To humans. To the world at large?" Nick asked.

"Especially if they're criminals," Dom said. "They'd be incredibly dangerous in that state."

"Which is why other pack's hunt and kill them. Lone wolves don't survive long. And in the time they are alive. They suffer. A lot. That's why it's considered such a severe punishment. Most wolves prefer a clean death as punishment for a crime."

"Gabriel was sending a message, then," Nick said.

"He was. The people of Eirene are off limits. Period."

"What about the wolves that helped Frank?" Dom asked. "The ones Mitch and I fought."

"They didn't directly harm or threaten a human. And Frank took the full blame for that crime. Fighting another shifter in neutral territory isn't necessarily a pack crime. So their punishment is for being associated with someone who threatened pack safety. They'll be caged and beaten for a month."

"Jesus," Nick said. "We lock up our own when they commit a crime. We don't beat them outside of an actual fight, certainly not when they can't defend themselves."

"Our world is harsh," Adam said with a shrug. "Especially when it comes to maintaining pack order."

Nick and Dom exchanged a look.

"And I thought our people were merciless about some things," Dom said.

Nick snorted. He frowned at Adam. "If Frank is now turned loose from the pack, what's to keep him from coming after Dom or Jane again? Why isn't he still a threat to us?"

"He can't get into our territory now," Adam said. "Think of it as alpha magic."

He smiled a little, and Dom and Nick nodded in understanding.

Shifters didn't really do magic in the conventional sense. Their natures were just what and who they were, no real magic involved. But pack-oriented shifters, like wolves, did have some tricks that could look like magic from the outside. Dom didn't know the details, and didn't care enough to ask, but he got the idea. Gabriel could literally prevent Frank from reentering his territory, by his power over the wolves as an alpha.

"Will that keep him out of my territory?" Nick asked.

"Not all of it, but most of it since your territory actually used to be part of ours and the transfer was done by money instead of wolf combat. Gabriel's influence is strong enough to cover most of this area—including Eirene. The town is safe now."

Dom let out a small sigh, his only outward show of relief. So long as she stayed in Eirene or was with him when she was outside of Eirene, Jane would be safe. He'd have to consider Ben's safety at college—Frank might be a threat to Ben in the future. But for now, the people Dom loved most were protected.

"Fair enough," Nick said. "But you should know, if he comes here again, if he finds a way back into Eirene, banishment won't be my punishment."

"He's fair game now," Adam said. And for the first time since entering the diner, he met Nick's gaze. "Kill him if you like. There won't be any retribution or consequences from us." He let his gaze slide away again after that, continuing to show deference to Nick.

Nick glanced at Dom. "What do you think? Good enough?"

"If I can kill him on sight without consequences," Dom said, "and if he's physically not allowed back into Eirene, I'm good with the punishment. For now."

"Gabriel would also like to make financial reparations for the threat to your mate," Adam said to Dom. "The only problem is, we're still in a bit of a financial bind after our last alpha."

Dom waved away the offer. "I don't need your money. Keep it to make your pack healthy. That'll pay me back more than money."

Adam's shoulders dropped with a release of tension. "Thanks."

Nick also relaxed his posture and leaned forward, his arms resting on the table. The mood of the meeting shifted from serious business to a friendly chat in that simple gesture. "Can I ask something that isn't my business, but I'm curious about now?"

"I'll answer if I can," Adam said.

"Your pack took in converted wolves who didn't have a pack, right? Chris' father brought in…lone wolves?"

"He did. They were abandoned by their creators, and usually hadn't asked to be changed."

"So would they suffer without a pack, the same way an outcast wolf would?"

"Exactly the same. Maybe worse because they'd have no idea why they're suffering since they don't understand their natures innately, the way a born wolf would."

"Is that why Doug Corwin took them in? To prevent them from going insane and endangering your whole species."

Adam smiled a little. "Doug was much more compassionate than your average alpha. Most alpha's kill rogue converted wolves that have been abandoned, working under the logic that they were abandoned because of some irredeemable characteristic that followed them into their wolf forms. Which makes them a threat. And threats are killed."

"Why did Doug take them in, then?" Nick asked. "If they were a threat."

"Some obviously remained a threat even after being taken in," Dom added, thinking of Frank.

"He thought they should be saved, helped. That no one was irredeemable and it was our responsibility to help them if we could because they didn't make the choice to become wolves."

"What if they had made the choice?" Dom asked.

"He would still take them in. He claimed that to abandon a wolf you've made is the height of cowardice, like abandoning one's entire pack if you were an alpha. He was big on people living up to their responsibilities."

"His efforts put his pack in jeopardy," Nick pointed out.

"Wouldn't have if his son had been a stronger alpha," Adam said. "If he'd been able to assert proper alpha control, rather than playing the 'bad boy' and giving the less civilized among our pack free rein." Adam sighed, his gaze wandering over the street outside the diner window. "We're still paying the price for letting Chris remain alpha for so long." He waved away the comment. "Anyway, you don't care about our problems."

"Only in how they affect my town," Nick said honestly.

"They shouldn't much anymore," Adam said. "Gabriel handing down a banishment has quieted most of the discord. At least for now."

"Good," Nick said. "I have to get back to the kitchen. You want something to eat?"

"I'm good. Thanks. Though, I am coming back the next time Lulu is on duty. Siobhan can't stop talking about the woman's sandwiches."

Nick chuckled.

Dom grinned at his brother when he said, "Better get one soon, before Nick decides to give Lulu her own restaurant."

Nick gave Dom a deadpan look. Adam laughed.

They watched the beta leave in silence.

"You think this took care of things?" Dom asked.

"Better have. I won't have any more trouble in my territory. Not now that Tiana and Chrissy are here." He glanced at Dom. "Not now that my brother is moving in and has a mate here."

Dom clapped Nick on the shoulder. "I'll back you up, no matter what."

"Always have. So what's next for you and Jane?"

"We have a date tonight. Dinner. Vail—your previous cook's restaurant?" Dom grinned when Nick rolled his eyes.

"I'll give her a call and see if I can get you a table tonight."

"Thanks," Dom said. "One more favor. Could you… invite Ben over? I know things are likely settled with the wolves and the threat is low, but it'll help Jane relax if she knows her boy is safe."

"Of course. We love Ben. I'll bribe him with homemade pizza, so he doesn't think we're trying to babysit him. He's been touchy about that since he turned eighteen."

"That'd be great." Dom had never been so grateful for his brothers before. They might have had a tough childhood, but they'd always had each other's backs, and he loved that he could still depend on Nick and Mitch, no matter what.

"So," Dom said. "Any thoughts on houses for sale?"

CHAPTER TEN

Jane was on the phone with Joe Sanchez when her front doorbell rang. She glanced at the clock. Exactly six o'clock. Dom was nothing if not punctual. She hurried down the stairs to the door, still finishing up her call.

"Thanks, Joe," she said as she opened the door, nodding Dom inside without looking at him too closely. "I'll be around tomorrow after my shift to pick them up." She hit the disconnect button on her cellphone, then looked up.

For a full forty seconds, she could only stare. She'd seen Dom looking all kinds of delicious and handsome before. She'd almost lost her resistance at Nick's wedding, seeing Dom decked out in a formal suit, the image of masculine beauty.

But tonight…

Tonight he literally took her breath way. His hair was neat but still a little shaggy—a look she loved on him. He was dressed more casually than he'd been at the wedding, wearing a pair of black slacks, a black button-up shirt, and a blazer-style coat. The solid black clothing brought out his light eyes, making them even more devastatingly arresting. Everything about his look was perfectly tailored to hit her in all her sensitive spots, and it was all she could do to keep her hands to herself.

"Wow," he said, blinking a few times.

She realized he looked as stunned as she felt, and preened at the knowledge. She glanced down at her dress— a simple navy piece that fit her curves snuggly and flared out around her knees in a flirty little hem. With three-quarter length sleeves and a skirt that fell below her knees, it wasn't exactly a scandalously flashy outfit, but the neck-line was cut low enough to show off her breasts without actually revealing much cleavage, and the fit left very little to the imagination. She felt super sexy in this dress, matched with a pair of nude heals, but she'd never had an excuse to wear it before.

She loved that Dom was her excuse now.

He swallowed visibly. "You look stunning. You wore your hair down."

She touched the waves, a little self-consciously. She almost always had her hair pulled back—in a tail or a bun or a braid, depending on the day. She kept it on the long side because it was easy and took very little effort, but she rarely let it loose because most of the things she did required her hair out of the way.

"And that dress," Dom said, his gaze moving over her body.

She tingled everywhere, and keeping her hands to herself got a lot harder.

"We have a seven o'clock reservation," he said, "but I'm sure I can push it back."

She laughed and smacked his hands away when he reached for her. "Dom Chernikov, you promised me a dinner that I didn't have to serve. Out at an actual restaurant. I'm holding you to that promise. Besides, I didn't waste all the time it took me to look like this just so you could undue it all the minute you stepped through the door."

"You're torturing me, then."

"Not on purpose." She grinned. "But it's a nice bonus. Been a long time since I've had a man look at me the way you are right now."

"Good. Any other man looks at you the way I am right now and I'm going to break his legs."

She shivered at the thrill his threat caused. Then cursed inwardly. What was it about that kind of aggressive maleness that turned her on so much? She definitely had a character flaw somewhere in her makeup.

She tried not to let that worry her. She wanted to believe he was different from her usual type. She wanted desperately to believe everything he told her. And for just a little while, she would.

She pulled a coat off the stand by the door and snatched up her purse. "Shall we go?"

He held her coat for her as she slipped into it, and her stomach clenched at the feel of his hands on her shoulders. When he leaned in and kissed her on the side of her neck, she almost forgot about going to dinner. He smelled all warm and masculine, like soap and aftershave, and it was an act of will not to turn into him and bury her face against his skin to savor that scent.

"You're sure I can't persuade you to delay dinner for an hour or so," he murmured against her temple.

Temptation had never felt so good. "No." But she sounded breathy when she said it. "Dinner first."

He nuzzled her neck again, the contact making her brain fuzzy and seriously playing havoc with her determination.

"Dinner first, then," he said. "But I'm having you for dessert."

Her knees almost buckled. She literally had to rely on his hold on her elbow to keep upright as they went down the stairs to the curb and his truck. That might have been embarrassing if anyone else had been around to see.

He held the truck door for her, helping her in with the kind of gentlemanly behavior that always made her feel special. As she buckled her seatbelt and waited for him to get in, she pressed her thighs together tightly, trying to calm some of the tingling tension. She was beyond turned on, and they hadn't actually been in each other's company for more than ten minutes.

How was she going to make it through dinner?

The drive to Vail could have been uncomfortable and yet wasn't. They chatted easily, something that surprised her for some reason. True, they'd known each other a long time, but after last night, after the tension before they'd left her house, she'd been worried conversation would be stilted. It wasn't. He kept things light, talking about movies, and music, the latest book Jane was reading, the game Ben was designing in his head, Tiana and Nick's baby, and the approaching family reunion.

He only brought up the werewolves long enough to tell her that her kidnapper had been punished and wouldn't be a problem anymore. When she started to worry, to consider whether or not she could trust that assertion, he stopped her before she got going and promised she and Ben would be safe. And God help her, she believed him. She couldn't look into his face and doubt.

Oh, she still intended to stock up on silver bullets. But more like the way she might keep a flashlight, water, and canned goods on hand in case of a storm—advanced preparation more than fear of the actual threat.

After that brief touch on the dangerous parts of the real world, Dom went back to talking about easy things that made her laugh. For the rest of the drive, she forgot to worry. And it was like a kind of miracle.

He took her to the restaurant of a former employee of Nick's—a woman chef so skilled, her restaurant was now getting international attention. Nick had helped the woman open the restaurant a couple of years ago, and if Jane hadn't already been fond of her boss, that would have cemented her loyalty.

"I haven't seen Kelly in a while," she told Dom as they waited by the front door for their table to be readied. "Hope she can come out and say hi."

Dom settled his hand at the small of her back as they moved between tables behind the maître de, and Jane thrilled at the protective gesture. Some men just had a way of making a woman feel sexy and feminine.

She didn't miss the other women staring at Dom—some of those women out with other men. But Dom never took his attention from her and didn't even seem to notice the stares. She almost laughed. The man was gorgeous, the kind of man who stopped women in their tracks in stunned amazement. Probably some men, too. And he wanted *her*. She wasn't sure she'd ever really get used to that thought.

Dinner was delicious, the conversation was easy, and Kelly did come out to say hi. Jane felt like a rock star, between the attention Dom drew and then having Chef Kelly stop at their table. She was used to observing people, gauging their moods, taking a quick assessment of their personalities. She saw it as part of her job to know how to deal with people, and that had served her well over the years. Now, she couldn't escape noticing the looks directed at her and Dom, the stares and quiet murmurs. She never would have suspected she'd like that kind of attention. But tonight, it was fun and flattering and a little bit naughty, like she was playing a part, getting to live in someone else's life for a few hours.

She could hardly believe this *wasn't* someone else's life.

As they left the restaurant, Dom kept a hand at the small of her back again, and Jane leaned into his touch, not sure she could have resisted him even if she'd wanted to.

"I'd ask if you wanted to go for a walk," he said near her ear, "but it's freezing, and I'm not sure I can wait much longer to get you naked."

Heat flooded through her already-humming system, right to her core, and it was on the tip of her tongue to point out that there were hotels all over Vail.

But that was the way she used to do things. Keeping her home life and her sex life completely separate. Never letting a man close enough to bring him back to her own house, even when she'd thought she'd avoided her usual bad choices and picked a nice man.

Things with Dom should be different. Were different.

Or at least she hoped they were different. Taking him back to her home was a way to prove it to herself.

"I'm not even remotely cold," she said, turning her face up to his. Her heels put her that much closer to his height, but he still had more than half a foot on her. She rose up on her toes and brushed her lips against his, torturing herself. "And a walk sounds lovely."

He groaned against her mouth and she almost laughed.

"But," she said.

He raised his head enough to meet her gaze.

"But I think we should get back to my place for dessert."

"Done." He fast-walked her to his car, his hurry making her chuckle.

It was also a relief. She couldn't wait much longer to get him into her bed.

They were barely through her front door before they pounced on each other. Coats, keys, purse, shoes, dropped onto the entryway floor as they kissed. His hands were gloriously rough, not even a hint of gentleness this time. And she gave as good as she got, ripping off one of his buttons in her hurry to get him out of his shirt.

"I am so turned on right now," she said against his neck. "I feel like I'm going to explode."

"Shut up or we'll never make it upstairs."

She bit his shoulder hard, loving his harsh groan and even harder hands on her ass.

Knowing Ben was safely ensconced at Nick and Tiana's house somehow made everything better. Her boy was safe, but somewhere else, so she and Dom had privacy. She could let go of any resistance or hesitance, and fuck Dom until neither of them could walk.

She lifted her skirt up to her hips, freeing her legs so she could jump up into Dom's arms and wrap herself around him. The move revealed the sexy stockings and garter belt she had on—a luxury she'd never anticipated wearing for a man; though if she were honest, she'd admit she'd been thinking about Dom when she bought them— and Dom's groan of approval left her beyond glad she'd splurged on the damned things. He kept one hand on her ass, holding her securely, and moved the other along the bottom of her thigh, his fingers toying with the edge of the stockings where the garter clipped onto the silk.

"These probably won't survive undamaged," he said, his voice deep and rough.

She shivered. "Fine by me. You can buy me another pair."

"Deal." And he flicked open the clasp holding the stocking.

So expertly, she narrowed her eyes at him. "Done that before, have you?"

He grinned, his only answer, before he kissed her again. Her suspicion died a fast death in that kiss. She didn't really care, couldn't care in that moment, because all she could think about was how wonderful he felt, all hard muscle and rough fingers, how hot and desperate she was for him, how delicious he smelled and tasted. And how much more of him she wanted.

"Upstairs," she ordered. "I want my mouth on your cock. Now."

"Fuck. Yes."

He was up the stairs so fast she gasped. For a little while tonight, she'd forgotten about the fact that he could turn into a tiger when he liked. The reminder of his speed and strength should have dropped her out of her lust-haze. It only made things worse. She couldn't get him naked fast enough.

He set her on her feet when they pushed into her bedroom, but when she started to reach for his pants, he stopped her and turned her to face the wall.

Leaning in close behind her, so she could feel the length of him along her back, he lifted her hands and set them against the wall.

"Don't move until I tell you to," he said against her ear.

She nodded, her throat too tight to actually speak.

He moved his hands along her arms, a long sweeping caress that started her nerves jumping. The sound of the dress' back zipper easing down was loud in the quiet room. He kissed the nape of her neck as he pulled her hands away from the wall long enough to slip her dress down her arms. The material pooled around her waist. Then he had her hands braced against the wall again, and his fingers found her bra clasp. She was very grateful for the support of the wall when his hands cupped her naked breasts. He pinched her nipples, kneading her until she moaned in complete surrender.

His lips glided over her nape, then down her spine as he moved his hands over her waist, to the dress still clinging to her hips. With a rough push, the material dropped to the ground. Then Dom dropped to his knees behind her, kissing the small of her back, flicking his tongue out at intervals, the unpredictable caresses making her jump and gasp.

She was so caught up in what his mouth was doing, she almost missed him opening her garters, only realized he had when he pushed her underwear down to her ankles. Slowly, he rolled each stocking down, holding her as she lifted each foot so he could remove the material. He pushed all of her clothing aside, then his hands were on her hips and his lips were gliding over her spine.

He fingered the garter belt still fastened around her hips. "This stays on. For a while longer."

She was too far gone to argue. She wasn't sure she could remember how to use words in that moment anyway.

Without meaning to, she arched her back, a gesture that pushed her ass closer to him, and he took advantage, trailing his lips over the curve of her butt, his hands caressing her stomach, low on her abdomen. The feel of his hands combined with the pressure of his mouth trailing over the sensitive skin along her ass was almost too much.

But she no longer had enough sense to do anything but let him control her body, giving him whatever he wanted because what he gave back in return was making her delirious.

He nipped her skin, hard enough that she gasped, and damned but she almost came.

She'd never felt like this before, so feminine and out of control and gloriously happy about it all. She felt safe, and desired, and sexy, and all the things she hadn't allowed herself to be in forever. She felt young, the tough years falling away so she could almost sense the kind of woman she might have been if she'd met Dom earlier, if she'd made better choices…

His tongue slid over her ass back up to her spine and she had to brace her legs to keep from dropping to the floor. He moved one hand between her legs, his fingers sliding through the slick wetness between her sensitive folds, and she cried out, so close to coming she could barely stand it.

He turned her around to face him where he knelt, gently pushed her back so she was leaning against the wall, and lifted one of her legs to brace over his shoulder. Then he licked into her. And she came, fast and hard. She was too primed, too ready, and she couldn't hold back. She cried out again, burying her hand in his thick hair, and let the orgasm roar through her like a fire, charging across her nerves in a mind-blowing explosion of a release that left her weak and panting and unable to stand on her own.

Which didn't matter because Dom didn't let her go, even when he stood. He picked her up and carried her to the bed, his eyes sparkling with lust and possessiveness.

She couldn't even think to argue with the possessiveness. He did own her in that moment, body and soul. And she didn't regret that even a little bit.

He settled her on the bed, coming down with her for a deep kiss that sent her floating on a luxurious cloud of desire. But as she ran her hands over his back, she hit his pants and realized he'd completely distracted her.

She pushed him up. "These slacks look superb on you," she said. "But they're coming off now or I'm gonna rip them off."

"Yes, ma'am."

She chuckled at his comment. Her thighs clenched at the deep sexy tone of his voice. He didn't waste time stripping out of his pants, and she enjoyed the sight of him, naked and aroused, hard and muscled. And for the moment, all hers.

"Get over here. I remember something about wanting your cock in my mouth."

"You're going to kill me."

"Not likely." She stroked the length of his erection as he climbed up on the bed next to her. "You look like a pretty strong guy."

He grunted something unintelligible and she took that as encouragement. Not that she needed any. Stroking him with one hand, she nudged him onto his back with the other, then she straddled his thighs. Ah, that felt good. She rubbed herself against his leg and savored the rough friction against her clit.

"You really do intend to kill me, don't you?" His voice

was so deep and gravelly now, it was like its own kind of caress.

"There's something you should understand about me, Dom," she said, lowering her head until her mouth was close to the tip of his cock. She licked out, catching just the very top in a quick taste, smiling when he sucked in a sharp breath. "I'm very selfish in bed. I want what I want, when I want it. Only what gives me pleasure." She tasted him again, and his back arched, his thigh muscles tightening under her. "You better be prepared to deal with that if you want to keep coming back to my bed."

"Whatever you want. Whenever you want it." He spoke through clenched teeth. "But I can't guarantee I won't take as much as I give."

"I'm counting on it." And she took him fully into her mouth.

She'd never admit it out loud, but she'd been thinking about sucking Dom since first meeting him, the way he might taste, the length of him, the texture. The reality was a pleasure and a turn-on that went way beyond what her imagination had invented. She licked the soft skin over hardness, sucked and savored and lost herself in exploring him. He trembled, his hands came into her hair, and she knew she was pushing him too far. But she didn't care. She'd warned him she was selfish. It was her turn to control his body and soul.

So she only lifted away when she knew he was on the verge of coming, giving him enough room to relax a little, before she went back to savoring his taste. Somewhere in her enjoyment, she realized if she let him come, while she'd enjoy that immensely, she'd miss out on taking him into her. Being able to fuck him without worrying about noise was a luxury she didn't want to waste.

He didn't argue when she finally released him, just helped her balance as she straddled his hips, then before she could slide down, he was slamming her hips against his, burying himself in her hard and fast and perfect. God the stretch of having him inside her was beyond any memory of sex she retained. Had it ever felt this good? Had she ever felt so connected and filled and satisfied?

She rocked against him, once, twice, then he took over and she loved that so much, she let him. The way he watched her body as he pumped into her made her dizzy. He looked at her like she was the most delicious, perfect woman he'd ever seen. And she'd never felt sexier, more beautiful. She didn't know how he did it, but at the moment she didn't care. She took everything he gave her, lapping it up like cream. His arm muscles flexed as he guided her hips, so strong and hard, she leaned over to brace herself on his shoulders, just to feel the muscles move. He half-sat and took one of her nipples between his teeth, the nip hard enough to make her gasp without it hurting.

He flipped her over, so fast she lost her breath. Braced above her now, he slammed into her, his gaze so intent on her, she couldn't look away from him. Not until that building tension in her core started to crest again. She tried to hold back, to watch him come, but the feel of him, hitting her in just the right spot, was too much. She closed her eyes and let go with a gasping scream of release. He went with her, pulsing inside her, crying out her name. The sounds of their release echoed in her bedroom for a long moment.

And Jane decided she liked that sound very much. Enough to want to keep hearing it for years.

That nagging voice that warned her she was about to make a mistake was quiet then, silenced by Jane's realization that any mistakes were already made. She'd lost the fight. The only way now was forward—even if the end of this road led to heartbreak.

Dom was still trembling, trying to recover from his orgasm, when he heard his cellphone ringing—downstairs in his coat pocket, on the floor somewhere in the entryway.

He groaned and set his forehead against Jane's. "My phone. I'd better go get it, in case it's Nick."

She kissed his nose and pushed him up. "I'm staying here because I can't walk yet."

"Good. You need to stay naked for a while longer anyway."

"Before you get ideas about another round, I need a nap first."

He chuckled, kissed her quickly, and hopped out of bed.

"You have one fine ass, Dom Chernikov," she said, her tone practically a purr.

Despite his recent release, his cock twitched at her compliment. "I'm pretty fond of yours too. I'll show you just how much when I get back."

She stretched, the movement raising her breasts, the sensuality of the move making his heart pound.

"I'll look forward to that demonstration," she said.

He didn't take the stairs so much as he jumped from the second floor landing to the first floor. It took another few minutes to find his coat in the piles of discarded clothes and shoes and then get his phone out of the pocket. The missed call list showed Nick's house number. He rang back, hoping the noise didn't wake Chrissy if she was asleep.

"You on the road?" Nick asked.

Dom frowned and glanced at the time on the phone. It was nearly midnight. Did Nick really think he'd spend that long over dinner when he had Jane all to himself and an empty bed waiting for them?

"No," he said, "we're back at Jane's. What's up? You need me to come get Ben?"

"He fell asleep on the couch. Didn't want Jane to worry. He can sleep here. We've got room and a sleeping baby— so long as that lasts."

"Thanks. How'd he do tonight?"

"Great. He seemed to think he was supposed to be babysitting Chrissy so we let him. He laid on the carpet in the living room next to her and played cooing games for more than an hour. Kid can really focus when he wants to."

"That he can. You sure you don't mind the house guest?"

"Na. He's good. Give our love to Jane. You two have fun."

Nick disconnected without waiting for a comment,

which was just as well because Dom might have said something rude in response to his older brother's innuendo.

He took the stairs two at a time, closing the bedroom door behind him. Jane was stretched out under the blanket now. And to his amusement, she was sound asleep. Guess she did need a nap.

He crawled into bed, settling under the covers next to her, and pulled her back against him, humming in approval when she snuggled tighter into his arms.

He still couldn't quite believe this was reality. That he had her in his arms, relaxed and sated. Her scent filled his head, surrounding him with her earthy essence and their love making. For the first time in a long while, Dom felt relaxed and comfortable in a soul-deep way, like he was exactly where he belonged.

That satisfaction went with him into a deep sleep filled with Jane's warmth and scent, imprinting her onto his soul.

CHAPTER ELEVEN

J ane woke with a start, and a moment of panic took her when she realized she'd slept in. The sun was bright through the crack in her curtains. Nick might have given her yesterday off, but she was still supposed to be in to work today.

And Ben? Where was he? Did he come home last night?

She rolled out of bed, and paused when she realized she was still naked. She faced the bed. Dom was reluctantly sitting up, rubbing his hands over his face.

He looked so good he took her breath away, and she forgot what she'd been doing.

Then she remembered Ben and went scrambling for a t-shirt and sweats in her dresser.

"If you're worrying about Ben, he spent the night at Nick's. He's fine."

She closed her eyes briefly, surprised she was surprised

he'd known what she was worrying about. "Thanks. That's what the phone call was about?"

"Yeah."

"You should have woken me up to tell me."

"Not after the last few days you've had. You needed your sleep."

She pulled her t-shirt over her head, then faced him. "I'm not used to people looking after me, you know. I'm the one who looks after others."

"Get used to it." He climbed out of her bed and came to stand in front of her, taking her shoulders in his hands. "There's nothing I want more in this world than the privilege of being able to look after you. If you argue with me about it, I will be deeply offended."

She rolled her eyes, made a face, and pretended not to be melting inside. "Fine. If you insist. I wouldn't want to be rude."

He snorted. "Right."

Then he pulled her close and kissed her, a kiss both gentle and intimate, and so so right.

She surfaced from the drugging effects of his good morning with a sigh. "I have work."

"I know. Shower and get dressed. I'll make you some breakfast."

"You don't have to…"

"What did I just tell you?" He glared at her, hands on his hips, looking for all the world like he was truly offended.

She forced down her grin and said, "Fine. Make breakfast. Be sure to make enough for yourself, too."

Then she disappeared into the bathroom so she wouldn't get lost in all her mushy feelings and forget what she was about.

He made her eggs and bacon again, enough to feed a small army. Which turned out to be good since Dom Chernikov could pack away a great deal of food.

"Wish I had your metabolism," she commented, shaking her head.

"It can be a pain. When I'm really focused and concentrating on work, I sometimes forget to eat. Then I have to devour an entire grocery store just to make up for it."

She laughed. "I'd pay money to see that show."

"Mitch and I were really grateful when Nick learned how to cook. Our uncle, who raised us, burned water."

"What did you eat before Nick started cooking?"

"Take-out mostly. That gets old after a few years."

"Years? Jesus, you're breaking my heart. Poor babies." She meant it too, because she thought of Ben, even with his picky eating habits, never getting a decent meal, and it made her heart ache.

"We got over it. I still can't eat Chinese food very often, but it gave Nick his vocation so it was worth it."

She toasted him with her coffee mug, then took a sip. He'd made the coffee strong and rich. Just the way she liked it.

"Your family descends today," she said, trying to stay level-headed while her heart did flip-flops and giddy, girly summersaults.

"Eirene will be overrun any moment. Which reminds me, I called Nick about you being a little late for work.

Ben's already at the restaurant eating breakfast and showing Charlie Sanchez how to play one of his favorite app games. Nick says he's never seen Charlie laugh so much—except when he's spreading gossip."

She grinned, then frowned. "I'm never late for work. Nick's gonna start docking my pay if I don't get back to my usual schedule."

"You know he won't."

"Still…" She didn't like the idea of falling in love and suddenly turning into a flake. Bad enough she'd gone and fallen in love. Every other relationship she'd been in had cost her something of herself. She'd worked hard at being dependable and solid over the years, especially here in Eirene. She'd feel pathetic if she turned into some silly mess just because she'd let Dom into her bed.

"You've started *thinking* again, haven't you?" he said.

She snorted. "You need to stop reading my mind."

"Your face gets all serious when you're thinking. And I can smell when you're worried."

"You can?"

He tapped his nose. "Tigers have a very good sense of smell, remember."

"Well, that's terrifying." He'd told her as much, but she'd forgotten about that detail. "What else can you smell?"

"Everything. Can't always parse out the feelings, but I can read your scent most of the time."

"So I haven't had any secrets from you ever, have I?"

"You have. But not your feelings. That's almost been the worst part of the last six years. Knowing you wanted me, even though you had no intention of giving me a chance."

"Damn."

She sipped her coffee again, wondering how to feel about that revelation. Guilt seemed wrong. She had nothing to feel guilty about. She couldn't help wanting him, but she'd done her best not to encourage his feelings. Not her fault he'd held out for so long.

Frankly, she was still a little awed that he had. No man had wanted her for so long with so little encouragement.

That sunk in, for the first time really penetrated her thinking. How different he was from all the other men in her life. She knew it, on some level, but didn't really trust herself enough to believe it. She wanted to, more than anything. But she was still having a hard time *knowing* this time would be different.

She looked at him across the table, at the slight quirk of his eyebrows because he knew she was thinking again. At the way his gaze held hers, steadily, without sliding away from her direct stare.

Maybe she could trust this. Maybe she could finally let go of the worry…

Maybe, for the first time in her life, she'd actually made a good choice in a man.

Which meant it might be the last time she had to make that choice. Ever again.

* * *

The diner was overrun with Chernikovs and their relations when Jane finally pushed through the front door. The clan matriarch, Elizaveta Chernikova sat at the counter flirting with Charlie, her Russian accent coloring her deep voice, her tone amused as Charlie smiled his gummy smile at her.

Alexis Tarasova and her husband Victor Romanov sat in a booth with a young woman Jane recognized as their daughter Isabella, along with Tiana and Chrissy. Isabella was cooing over the table at the baby, making her giggle. The sound charmed Jane—she'd always been a sucker for baby giggles.

She headed toward the kitchen to drop her coat and purse and put on her apron. She waved to Mitch, sitting in the booth behind Alexis and Victor, holding hands across the table with his fiancée. Jane liked Nila De Luca, though she'd only met her the one time at Nick's wedding—a smart, no-nonsense kind of woman who seemed to keep Mitch on his toes. Given the charm the youngest Chernikov brother wielded, Jane was glad to see he'd found a woman who could keep him in line.

She ducked into the kitchen, taking in Nick's busy grill in a glance as she headed into the breakroom. "Be on the floor in a sec," she told him. "Sorry I'm late. Won't happen again."

"Don't worry. Ben's been helping pour coffee."

"He has?" She paused to stare at Nick. "The crowd hasn't bothered him?"

The diner could get pretty busy during the day, but

when Ben was around during the busy times, he usually stayed at the counter and played on his tablet or talked to a local he knew well. He wasn't shy with people at all, but he did still tend to get overwhelmed by a lot of strangers. Or at least, he had before he'd left for college.

"He's grown a lot since he started college," Nick said, echoing her thoughts. "He doesn't talk a lot when he's pouring coffee for strangers, but he's making the rounds with my family without any trouble at all."

"Huh." Her heart got that strange tightening-swelling sensation, so full of love and relief it was overwhelming. She shook off the moment and went into the breakroom to put her coat and purse into her locker and get out her gear for her shift.

Back out on the floor, she noticed Ben hovering near the table with Tiana and the baby, smiling shyly at Isabella as she played peekaboo with Chrissy. Jane almost went over to tease him about already having a girlfriend but decided not to just yet. For all he was turning into an adult before her eyes, she didn't want to be that mom who embarrassed him in front of other people. She'd save her teasing for when they got home.

She did stop by to kiss him on the cheek, though. She greeted everyone at the table and thanked Tiana for letting Ben stay the night.

"He can stay any time," Tiana said. "I actually got to take a nap while he played with Chrissy. It was wonderful."

Jane chuckled. "I warned you what you'd be getting into, being a parent."

Tiana grinned. "You were right. About it being worth everything, too."

Jane brushed a gentle caress over Chrissy's head, savoring the lovely baby smell. "I'd better get back to work. You all need anything?"

"We're good. Thanks," Tiana said. Before Jane could walk away, though, she said, "You're coming to dinner tomorrow night, right? Up at Elizaveta's rental?"

"Am I? Hadn't heard about it."

"Dom didn't tell you? He probably forgot. You're invited. You and Ben both. Please, come. It wouldn't be a family gathering without you two."

Jane's throat tightened. She smiled and nodded. "We'll be there, if you want us. Thank you."

"I'll babysit more," Ben said. "Chrissy likes me."

Jane kissed him on the cheek again and went back to work, but her throat was still tight with all the emotions rioting through her. She'd always felt at home in Eirene, accepted and liked. The town had become her family, a family she was protective of. But this sense of being taken into the Chernikov family went a step beyond that, like the extended family she'd never really missed having and now couldn't imagine being without.

She'd lose all that if Dom broke her heart. If she broke his.

It was only just hitting her how much that would hurt, beyond the usual guilt and shame over a relationship mistake. If things went wrong with Dom, she'd lose more than just a lover. She'd lose a family. Oh, she'd lost her parents when she'd run off with Ben's father. But somehow, this seemed worse, more painful. Because these were people she'd chosen as her family. People she *wanted* in her and Ben's lives.

Damn. What had she done?

Fortunately, between the lunch rush and the various members of Nick and Tiana's families coming and going from the diner all afternoon, Jane didn't have too much time to think about the future. She focused on the tasks at hand, enjoyed the buzz and energy of her work, and made sure no one's drink cup went empty.

She blinked in surprise when her shift ended. The time had gone so fast, she'd barely noticed.

Dom was supposed to meet her at her house later that evening. He had to move from his motel room to the house Elizaveta had rented but said he'd call and arrange a time to meet once he was settled. He wanted to treat her and Ben to dinner and a movie and she'd been beyond pleased with his offer to include Ben. She was still adjusting to mixing her dating life with Ben, but somehow with Dom it all seemed natural and normal. Like they'd been a family for longer than she cared to admit.

Ben had gone home hours earlier, leaving her to walk back alone after a quick stop at the pharmacy to collect the additional ammunition Joe had made for her. She pulled her coat tight around her shoulders as she strolled up her street, admiring the Christmas lights decorating some of the houses, enjoying the snow-cold air. She didn't trust the joy bubbling through her veins, but she savored it anyway. Because it felt too wonderful and right.

She spent more than half an hour staring at her closet, trying to decide what to wear and feeling silly doing it. She was too old to act like this, but it felt so damned good to be worrying over something as simple as what outfit to wear on a date that she didn't care. Ben came out of his room to help her choose between jeans and slacks—he had some very definite opinions on her wearing jeans on a date, all of which were that she shouldn't. She was so charmed by her son helping her get ready, she let him pick her outfit.

As the evening descended, though, and she hadn't yet heard from Dom, worry started to pierce that bubble of happiness she'd been walking in. She didn't want to jump to any conclusion, but that ugly, gloating voice in the back of her mind kept whispering that Dom was done with her, that she'd made another bad choice and now both she and Ben would suffer for it.

Irritated at herself, she picked up her cellphone and just called the man.

She called him five times with no answer. The voice-mail didn't even come on. Next she tried the motel, just to see if Dom had checked out yet. Diane Leibowitz, an Eirene resident and regular diner customer, was working the front desk. She told Jane it didn't look like Dom had checked out, but she'd only been on the desk for a few hours so he might have left before she started her shift since the previous person manning the desk was really bad at the paperwork.

Jane wasn't sure whether to be worried, angry, hurt, or

offended. Swallowing some combination of all those emotions, she tried Nick's house number. No answer so she tried his cell.

He answered on the second ring. "Hey, Jane. What's up?"

"Where are you?"

"Up at Elizaveta's rental, why?"

"Dom there with you? Has he moved up there yet?"

"Haven't seen him since yesterday. Just a second." He muffled the phone but she heard him call out to someone nearby. After a few minutes, he came back on the line. "No one's seen him."

There was a pause Jane didn't like, one filled with questions and no answers, a tension she couldn't read.

"He was supposed to call me this afternoon," she said. "I haven't heard from him. Tried his cellphone and no answer. No voicemail."

"Not even a voicemail? That's…unusual. Maybe he just went for a run and he's out of cell range."

"Did he leave, Nick?" she asked quietly. "Is he gone?"

"Jane, he spent yesterday asking me about houses for sale in Eirene. He hasn't left you."

She swallowed hard, forcing down the emotions threatening to choke her. "So I'm worrying about nothing?"

"Probably." Another of those pauses. "I'll swing by the motel and check on him. He probably got to working and lost track of time. Or he went for a run or something."

"I called the motel. He hasn't checked out. Nick…" She bit her bottom lip and looked down the stairs, hoping Ben couldn't hear her. He was in the living room with his tablet so he likely wasn't listening, but… She went into her bedroom and closed the door. "Nick, Dom told me the wolves weren't a problem anymore. Did he lie so I'd feel better? Should I be worried?"

"He wasn't lying but…" Nick's pause lasted a little longer this time. Then he cursed. "The motel is outside my territory."

"Your what?"

"My territory. And the wolves… Fuck. I'm going to the motel. I'll call when I know something."

"Don't think for even one minute you're going there without me," she said. "I'll meet you there."

"Ben…"

"Damn it." He had her there. She didn't want to leave Ben alone if the wolves were still a problem.

"Jane, this could be nothing. Don't worry. I'll check on him and make him call you immediately. Okay. I'll take care of it."

He disconnected without letting her respond. But she hadn't missed the worry in his voice, and her own ratcheted up to new levels. She was good at worrying, and she was doing it now with Olympic-level skills.

She took her shotgun from the top shelf of her closet along with the lockbox with her silver ammunition. Then she pulled on a ski jacket with plenty of pockets, filled them with the shotgun cartridges, and headed downstairs, still wondering what to tell Ben and how to make sure he was safe…

He looked up when she walked into the living room, saw the shotgun, and frowned. "What's wrong?"

"Dom's not answering his cell. I'm meeting Nick at the motel to check on him. Only…" She frowned. Her boy hated being treated like a child, and she knew she had to let him grow up, but she also needed to protect him more than she needed just about anything else in the whole world.

"Sheriff Smith asked me to come by his office to fix his email," Ben said, standing and setting aside his tablet. "He claims it's acting up on its own, but I think he screwed it up and doesn't want to admit it. I told him I couldn't work on it until tomorrow cause of the movie with Dom, but I can go now."

She leaned the empty shotgun by the door and pulled her son in for a hug. "Thank you for understanding how much I need you to be safe."

"You, too, Mom." He leaned back, but wouldn't quite meet her gaze. "Be careful. Stick with Nick. He can look after you if something is wrong."

"I can look after myself." She nodded back to the gun. "And if Dom's in trouble, I have to help."

"You think he's in trouble?"

"Maybe. Maybe he just got caught up in work and forgot the time. Maybe his cellphone battery is dead and he hasn't noticed."

"I do both those things."

"I know. Everything could be just fine."

"You don't think it is, though."

"I'm worried."

"You worry a lot."

She smiled and cupped his cheek. He was as tall as her now, almost taller. And when she paused to really look at him, she saw the man he was becoming instead of the boy she remembered so well. The beauty of that was bittersweet.

"Yes," she said. "I probably do worry too much. But just in case, I'm going to check on Dom, and I need you safe while I do. I'll drop you at the sheriff's on my way to the motel."

Where she hoped with everything in her that she'd find Dom, safe and busy and forgetful. With fear pounding on her chest, she could even forgive him for simply leaving her. She'd swallow her pride and accept another bad choice, just so long as he was safe.

CHAPTER TWELVE

Because she'd been coming from home and Nick had to get all the way down a mountain and across town from Elizaveta's rental, Jane arrived at the motel at the same time as him. He stalked toward her as she climbed out of her car, scowling so fiercely, she might have been afraid if she didn't know the man so well.

"I told you to stay home," he said.

She reached back into her car, pulled out the shotgun, cracked it open, and slid in two of the cartridges loaded with silver buckshot. "And I told you, I wasn't letting you come here to check on him without me."

"What about Ben?"

"At the sheriff's fixing his emails. Which room is Dom's?"

Still scowling, Nick cursed under his breath and led the way.

They passed between the thick wooden planting boxes lining the edge of the parking lot, separating it from the walkway in front of the motel's first-floor room doors. Pine and fresh snow and the faint hint of gasoline from the nearby highway hung in the air, all familiar smells of home to Jane.

Dom must have had a ground-floor room since Nick walked away from the external staircase leading up to the two levels above and stayed on the sidewalk heading toward the far end of the motel. Jane glanced toward the main building with the check-in desk where Diane was still on duty. No one seemed to be around, or paying any attention to them.

As they got closer to the rooms at the far end of the building, Jane realized the way this part of the motel angled slightly away from the main building made these rooms hard to see from the check-in desk. Unless they were paying attention, the staff could easily miss Dom coming and going from his room.

Nick paused just outside the second-to-last door and started cursing again.

Jane scooted around him to see what he was looking at. There was a dark stain on the concrete that looked like blood and next to it was a room key.

Her heart started to thud so fast and hard it stole her breath. "Jesus. Tell me that's not blood."

"It's blood," Nick said, running a hand through his hair. "Dom's blood. And I can smell wolf."

* * *

Dom came too with a groggy groan, but when he reached up to rub his head, he heard a clank and found he couldn't lift his hand past his sternum. That realization brought him awake fast.

He scanned his surroundings with his senses as he tried to piece together what had happened. He was sitting on the wooden floor of what might have been a cabin, his wrists bound in thick metal cuffs attached to even thicker chains. He gave them an experimental tug—most ordinary chains couldn't hold a tiger shifter. Unfortunately, he realized after a few good jerks, these were not ordinary chains. The alloy was clearly strong enough to hold out against his shifter strength.

What in the fucking hell had happened?

He squinted and blinked a few times to clear the spots in his vision, then studied the room around him. It was a mostly bare space with a single wooden table against the far wall, wooden floors, wooden walls, and a single door opposite him with some substantial looking locks. There was an overhead bare bulb, the only light inside the room, and the spots he assumed were windows were covered over by curtains. No light leaked past the cracks in the curtains, which meant either they were boarded over or it was well past sunset.

Sonofabitch. *Jane*!

His head pounded, but he forced away the irritating pain and concentrated, thinking back to the last things he remembered clearly—breakfast with Jane. Dropping her off at work before heading back to the motel… He had some work to do, mostly paperwork and going over the payroll, before he checked out and moved his stuff up to Elizaveta's cabin. He'd avoided going into the diner so he wouldn't get caught up in family before he could get his work done.

He had a vague memory of pulling the motel key out of his coat pocket…

And then a blinding pain in his head that was followed by nothing but blackness.

As he tried to pull up anything that might explain all this, the subtle scents in the room finally separated out and made themselves known—cedar, oak, the nostril-irritating scent of bleach…and wolf.

A lot of wolves had been through this place, but most of those smells had been faded by time. The strongest, most recent scent came from one very specific wolf with a grudge.

Dom cursed, low and eloquently. The motel was outside Nick's territory, and it was outside the parts of the wolf territory Dom had always avoided to honor the deal Nick had made with the former alpha. But Dom had assumed the area around the motel was part of the wolves' extended territory, the places the alpha could control.

Stupid, arrogant mistake.

He jerked on the chains again, straining against their solid resistance. He was a lot more irritated than scared. If Frank had to chain him, it meant the bastard knew Dom could and would kill him. Frank had ambushed Dom this time, rather than call him out to a fight like he'd done the night he'd kidnapped Jane. The bastard didn't want a fair fight now. He wanted revenge, and he knew a regular challenge match wouldn't do it.

Dom snarled and cursed again. If the asshole wolf thought chains were going to save him from Dom's anger, he was very wrong. Dead wrong.

But Jane…

Dom's gut tightened as fear bit down hard. She was his biggest vulnerability and the wolf knew it. What if Frank somehow managed to lure Jane away from Eirene? What if she went to the motel looking for Dom and the wolf was waiting for her, the way he'd waited for Dom?

Fuck. Panic shot through him as fast as it had the night Ben called for help. He jerked harder at the chains, hard enough that the cuffs cut into his wrists and the chain bolts imbedded in the thick walls behind him stretched. They didn't break, but now that Dom realized what was happening, he also knew these chains wouldn't hold him for long —they were for wolves, made with silver threaded through them. Designed to hold a different beast.

Dom stared at the door, letting his senses of smell and hearing take in all the surroundings, letting his tiger sort through everything for the valuable information, as he pulled at the cuffs around his wrists. While a werewolf wouldn't be able to shift with his wrists wrapped in silver, the silver was no impediment to a tiger shifter. Dom could let his tiger out and slip free of the cuffs easily enough while he was mid-shift.

But even at his fastest, it still took a few minutes to

change fully, and while he was in the middle of shifting, he'd be easy prey to the wolf.

That might have even been the bastard's plan. Dom couldn't be sure if Frank was working alone now that he'd been banished or if he still had other wolves helping him. Dom couldn't smell anyone beyond Frank, but that didn't mean there weren't more wolves out there somewhere that hadn't come into the cabin yet. It was possible someone was just waiting to enter this room and kill Dom mid-shift. Though if they'd wanted him dead, they could have killed him while he was unconscious.

Dom could barely think logically around his fear for Jane, but he tried to force his mind to work. Though wolf musk permeated the place, he could only smell Frank strongly. The longer he focused, the more Dom could smell under all that dog-stench, wood and bleach. There was a definite metallic flavor, a coppery scent of blood. His lip curled almost reflexively. The scent of blood called to the predator in him, bringing his tiger to the surface.

What the hell had happened here? Where was *here* exactly? This was obviously a wolf place, but it had to be outside pack territory or Frank couldn't have brought Dom here.

He stretched his senses to their edge, looking for signs of Frank or any other wolves beyond the cabin. He couldn't sense or scent anyone nearby but that wasn't a guarantee none were in the area. A tiger could smell other shifters, but Dom couldn't sense them the way he did his own people, beyond a sort of vague otherworldliness when another shifter was close. And a werewolf could lay in wait, upwind, outside Dom's ability to sense, smell, or hear, and still move fast enough to reach the cabin while Dom was in the middle of his change.

It was a risk he had to take. He needed to get out of here. He had to get back to Jane.

He let out a long slow breath, turning his focus to the change, letting the shift take him. His clothes shredded as his body contorted, bent and broke, reformed from the inside out. His face stretched and moved, fur covered his arms.

He was well past the point of being able to stop, his tiger rolling over his human form, taking over, when the cabin door slammed open.

Frank stood in the doorway, grinning, and all Dom could do was roar as his tiger rushed to get free.

* * *

Jane bent and retrieved Dom's dropped room key as Nick sniffed the area. "We should check his room," she said.

"He didn't make it inside."

"How can you tell?"

"Hard to explain. The way things smell, the position of the key. Dom hadn't gotten it near the lock yet."

"Still… I'm checking." She opened the door, not even a little guilty about invading Dom's privacy.

The room was neat, the bed made, his clothes put away

except for a pair of jeans hanging over the back of the desk chair. She hunted through the room, just in case, found the safe locked, the bathroom empty, the message light on his phone blinking, and no signs of trouble.

"Nothing," she said stepping back outside.

"It's Frank," Nick said, his voice a little distracted and distant. "Not smelling any others…" He pulled out his cell-phone and dialed someone.

Jane tapped her foot, waiting impatiently as panic swelled in her throat. She had to do something, find Dom, save him…

Jesus, was this what he'd felt when she'd been taken? It was a wonder he hadn't ripped Frank apart. Because she intended to do just that if he'd so much as wrinkled Dom's shirt. The fact that Dom's blood was on the ground, too much to be a good thing but fortunately not enough to mean Dom was dead—

At least, she hoped not. She stared at Nick, wanting to ask but not wanting to interrupt, especially when she heard him ask for Gabriel Walsh—that was one of Siobhan's brothers. A werewolf.

Nick stared at her as he spoke to the other man, telling him what had happened quickly. He listened, cursed, then hung up.

"Come on," he said to Jane. "We'll take my truck."

"Where are we going?"

"The wolves have a place… I'll explain on the way."

She climbed into his truck, settled the shotgun on her lap, the barrel pointed toward the door, the safety on, then pulled out her cell. One of theirs was in trouble. Time to call in the cavalry.

* * *

Dom was dimly aware of the wolf stalking closer to him, but he was on the edge of full tiger now and couldn't defend himself. He pushed his shift, the adrenaline of fear and anger sending him into his tiger form faster than any time before—other than when he'd raced into the woods to rescue Jane. That thought pushed him through the last changes, his body settling into his tiger shape just as Frank reached him.

But before Dom had a chance to adjust to his new form, the wolf punched him in the side with a long metal stick—a cattle prod that sent a bolt of electricity through Dom.

His body jerked out of his control, landing him flat on his stomach. The shot of electricity was so strong, it locked his jaw and he couldn't even roar.

"Poor little kitty," Frank said, and punched him with the stick again.

This bolt made Dom's limbs buck and he bit his tongue, despite his jaw being too tight to open. Frank smirked and paced a few feet away, watching Dom as he panted and tried to force his limbs to work.

"Hurts, doesn't it?" Frank said. "Doug used this on the strays he collected." He gestured to the cabin. "Outside pack territory. On purpose. Designed to hold us converted strays. If the alpha took us into pack territory, it was as good as agreeing to accept us. Couldn't have that until we agreed to accept him as alpha. So he brought us here first. All of us."

Since Dom was in tiger form, he couldn't have answered even if he wasn't still trembling from the electrical shocks. His limbs stung and his nerves jumped, but he could almost make his paws move so he focused on that, concentrating on getting his body back under his control.

"That old alpha bastard tortured us until we gave in to his domination," Frank continued. "Then he made like a magnanimous leader by taking us into his pack."

The wolf settled in the chair at the table, staring in Dom's direction though his gaze was distant.

"When Doug finally died and Chris took over, things got a lot better for wolves like me. Chris knew how to run a pack."

Dom grunted and managed to get his legs under him so he could roll onto his stomach. He still couldn't stand, but at least he could move on his own again.

Frank's gaze sharpened and he smiled. "You'll find the cuffs have tightened. Can't just slip those big paws out now."

Dom snarled down at the silver bands still tight around his forepaws. His tiger wrist was a lot thicker than his human wrist, and the cuffs now bit into him, through fur and skin, making it difficult to move his paws at all. The electrical current sent through his body had heated the metal, and Dom smelled scorched skin and fur as well as blood. He licked at the area around the hot cuffs, to speed his already fast healing. But he wouldn't get the damned cuffs off now.

"Thought you'd be able to slip out during a shift, didn't you?" Frank smirked. "Probably could have without me distracting you." He laughed. "The look on your misshapen face when I walked in." He snarled and leaned forward, the cattle prod held casually in his hands where they rested on his spread knees. "Feel that fear, kitty cat? That's only a hint of what I'm going to make you feel."

Dom lifted his lip in a snarl, hissing a warning. Even with the damned cuffs on, the chains wouldn't keep his tiger contained for long. While a werewolf was significantly bigger than a regular wolf, it still wasn't as big as a full-grown male Amur tiger—and not quite as strong. Tiger shifters might look more like their natural animal counterpart than a werewolf, but the tiger shifters were significantly stronger.

Without making it obvious, Dom leaned forward, ensuring the chains were stretched tight. He jerked his back legs in a spasm-like movement, letting Frank think he was still suffering under the effects of the cattle prod.

Frank watched him with a slight smile, his dark eyes glittering. "Are you worried for your woman?" he asked quietly. "She's next. I'll bring her here while you're still alive, but too fucked up to help her. Then you can watch me fuck her, and bleed her, and choke the life out of her. All while knowing there's nothing you can do about it."

Dom narrowed his eyes, his tiger focused on prey now, his body still and controlled, waiting to pounce. The chains stretched tighter as he inched his body forward a little more.

Frank stood suddenly and punched Dom with the cattle

prod again, sending another breath-stealing shot of electricity into his limbs. Fucking hell! Dom's body convulsed again, robbing him of all the advantage he'd gained.

"Now, kitty," Frank said, squatting down so he could look Dom in the face. "What shall we play with first? The knife? Or the ax?"

CHAPTER THIRTEEN

Nick reached out and stopped Jane mid-call. "What are you doing?"

"Calling the sheriff. We need backup."

"Do you want to put more humans in danger? I can take care of the wolf. Gabriel and Adam are on their way, too." He released her hand to focus on his driving. "Frank's likely got Dom at a cabin outside wolf territory, where their former alpha…their leader used to keep stray wolves before bringing them into pack territory."

Jane stared at the side of Nick's face. "Most of what you're saying makes absolutely no sense."

He waved a hand in the air. "It's all a wolf thing. I don't know enough about it to explain it. What you need to know is that the bastard who kidnapped you was banished from the werewolf pack and, according to the current leader, that's a punishment worse than death. It also means he can't come back inside any of the pack territory. But the damned motel is outside both mine and pack territory."

"And this cabin we're going to?"

"Also outside pack territory. Which is why Frank can go there and why Gabriel thinks that's where they are."

She raised a hand. "The details are confusing me. Just tell me why I can't call in the sheriff."

"Frank is a lot more dangerous now that he's been banished."

"Doesn't sound like he got much of a punishment then."

"It is for a wolf. Apparently. He wasn't supposed to be a threat to any of the humans in Eirene because he can't get anywhere near the town now. Gabriel gave me the impression Frank wouldn't survive long after being outcast."

"Survived long enough to hurt Dom."

Nick snarled and grunted. "And that will be something the alpha and I *discuss* after we get Dom back."

She swallowed hard, afraid to say this out loud, but she had to. "He might have already…" She couldn't say it. She just couldn't.

Nick glanced at her. "If all he'd wanted was to kill Dom, he would have done it at the motel. The fact that he took him somewhere means the wolf is looking to torture Dom."

"Well that's not good!"

"But it means Dom will still be alive. We just have to get to him."

"Speed the hell up then. And you still haven't said why I shouldn't call in the cops."

"First, this is outside their jurisdiction so they can't officially do anything."

"That's not the real reason."

Nick snorted. "I don't want the sheriff—or anyone else for that matter—outside of Eirene until I've killed Frank."

"You don't want to get arrested for killing Frank either."

"Doubt the sheriff would bother. But that's another point."

"What if I kill Frank?"

He glanced at her. "Same argument. Dom would kick my ass if I let you get arrested. Or hurt. Which means you need to do everything I tell you when we get there."

She raised her brows.

"Jane, I mean it. You aren't used to the shifter world. You have to listen to me or you'll get hurt. I can't have that."

"I'm good with my shotgun," she pointed out.

"Bullets don't work well on werewolves."

"Silver ones do."

He frowned. "You have silver bullets."

"Nick, we know about werewolves. Of course we have silver bullets."

"What, everyone?"

"Everyone in Eirene with a gun."

"Well hell. Why didn't I know all this?"

She shrugged. "You weren't paying enough attention."

He scowled at her. She stared back. He shook his head and focused on his driving again.

"If we can't call the sheriff," she said, "why don't we call in your family?"

He hesitated for long enough, Jane narrowed her eyes at him. He glanced at her and winced.

"I don't want Tiana to know. Okay. I have Mitch keeping her busy so she doesn't notice anything is wrong."

"She won't take kindly to you trying to wrap her up in cotton wool like that, you know?"

"Which is why I don't want her to know about this, so don't tell her. She'd come rushing in to help, and I don't want her anywhere near danger right now. Not while she has Chrissy to protect. That's her job. I can take care of the damned wolf on my own."

"You're so confident you don't need help, why are you taking me?"

He gave her a deadpan glance. "You've already proven you'll just follow me even if I try to leave you behind. Better to have you where I can keep an eye on you." He glanced down at the shotgun in her lap. "Besides, you came prepared."

She snorted at that. "Damn straight."

They turned off the highway onto a dirt road. Without the sporadic highway lights, the forest was pitch black. She couldn't see a thing beyond Nick's headlights—and realized even if she'd called the sheriff, she wouldn't have known where to send him.

"You sure you know where you're going?" she asked.

"We're almost there." He waved at her gun. "How much ammunition do you have?"

"My pockets are full. But I only need one clean shot."

He slowed as the truck bumped over uneven dirt. They were climbing to a higher elevation, the rough road moving at a sharper angle the farther they went into the woods. Jane squinted out the side window, trying to see into the trees, but mostly she just saw blackness.

"You have good night vision?" she asked Nick.

"Excellent. And on that note…"

What little light there'd been from his headlights went out. Jane gasped and faced him. "What the hell?"

"We're almost to the place we'll need to park. Frank will hear us coming if we try to drive any closer. I need to let my eyes adjust to the dark."

She realized as her own eyes adjusted, the packed snow between the trees did reflect a little light, but not enough for her to see well. "Is there a long way to go?"

"Not too far. I can carry you and move quicker. Or you can wait here."

"Well that last part's not happening."

He snorted an almost laugh. Then he stopped the truck in the middle of the road.

"No one's likely to be coming this way—except Gabriel and Adam. And there's nowhere to pull off that isn't covered with deep snow." He looked at her, taking in her thick ski jacket, jeans and boots. "You're going to get cold on the run."

"I can take it. Let's go. My gut is churning, worrying about Dom."

He climbed out without another world. She circled the truck to join him, where he stared into the trees.

"What if they're not here?" she asked, afraid to hear the answer.

"I can sense Dom," Nick said. "They're here. Dom will know we're coming."

"And the wolf?"

"Depends on his sense of smell." He took her shotgun then turned and squatted down a little, motioning her up onto his back. "Come on. We've got some ground to cover."

"Haven't had a piggyback ride since I was eight."

He snorted as she settled with her legs around his waist and her arms around his shoulders. "Hold tight. Keep your eyes closed so you don't get disoriented."

"Yeah, I remember that."

She squeezed her eyes tight and pressed her forehead into his shoulder. She still gasped when he leapt forward and had to grip tighter to keep from falling off. The air bit sharp and cold against her bare hands as they moved through the trees, but she kept her eyes firmly shut and counted slowly in her head, concentrating on reaching Dom before it was too late.

Frank went to a corner of the room where shadows had concealed an ax leaning against the wall. He hefted the tool in one hand, swinging the big, heavy thing like it weighed nothing. Then he looked over his shoulder at Dom and smiled.

Dom's gut tightened. Tigers could heal from a lot of

damage but a severed limb was gone. They didn't regrow body parts once they were cut off like some shifters could. He snarled, an instinctive reaction, and though he was still trembling from the last bolt from the cattle prod, he scrambled against the wooden floor, trying to get his feet under him so he could stand and face the threat.

Frank chuckled. "I like that, kitty. I like smelling your fear." He stalked closer, carelessly swishing the ax back and forth at his side. "Got any idea what it's like not to have a pack? Like there's something crawling under your skin. Makes you want to tear and bite and claw the little fuckers out. Except there's nothing there to get out."

Casually, as if he was poking Dom with a stick instead of a weapon, Frank applied the cattle prod to Dom's side, sending another punch of electricity through him. This time, Frank held the prod in place, burning the hair and skin under it. Dom roared, the sound loud in the enclosed cabin, but he couldn't move away from the damned prod.

Frank's eyes gleamed, faintly yellow. "Smells like barbecue in here now. Wonder what kitty meat tastes like."

Dom barely heard him through the pain racking his body. He felt like he was on fire, burning from the inside out and his tiger roared again as the shock dragged Dom's logic under his animal's instincts.

Even after Frank pulled the prod away, Dom couldn't control his limbs. The burns on his side started to heal immediately, but the heat and pain still robbed him of breath. Panting, his jaw tight, he struggled to make his body work, to get his legs under him. He had to get out of this. Frank had threatened his mate. If he couldn't get free, Jane might be hurt.

The thought sent adrenaline racing through his system, scattering the pain fast. He forced his muscles to work, using the momentum of trying to sit up to jerk at the chains. He felt one bolt start to give. He lunged forward, with as much strength as he could manage, and that bolt gave way, freeing one of his legs from the wall.

Frank, who'd stalked away, swung back to face him. "Strong kitty. Guess you need a little more heat."

He leapt forward and shoved the cattle prod into Dom's shoulder. Dom roared and fought, but his body jerked out of his control again. Spots danced in his vision, the cabin filled with the smell of burnt skin and hair, rancid in the tight confines. Frank laughed and swung the ax up high, dropping it into the wood in front of Dom's nose.

"Oops, missed," Frank said.

Dom knew he'd missed on purpose, a part of him recognizing Frank wanted Dom to experience the dread of what would happen as much as he wanted to physically hurt Dom. As his tiger took over more and more of his thinking, Dom realized Frank's ploy was working. He could almost feel the ax cutting into his limbs, anticipated the pain and shock without Frank having to do more than threaten. He struggled against the remaining chain, panic starting to edge in past his anger and fear for Jane. Pure, animal panic.

And then the door to the cabin exploded inward, shattering into splinters of sharp wood.

Dom's panic was so strong, he'd never even sensed

Nick's approach. But there was his older brother, crouched in the middle of the cabin's bare floor as the remains of the door settled around him. Nick was in his human form, but his eyes glowed in the unforgiving illumination from the cabin's single bare bulb.

Frank faced the threat, snarling. "More kitties to play with. Come on, you fucker." He swung the ax with one hand, a wide arc that sliced the air in front of him, and held out the cattle prod in his other.

Dom struggled to get his body working again as his brother distracted the wolf. Nick didn't have any weapons, just his hand-to-hand fighting skills, and while those were significant, they weren't going to help if he got incapacitated from the damned electrical prod. Dom jerked at the remaining chain still holding him to the wall, pulling hard and long as the bolt started to give.

While he was still struggling to free himself, a scent reached him through the remains of the door. Jane! No. What was she doing here? The wolf would smell her, use her again. Dom roared and jerked at the bolt, the thick metal finally giving.

Dom lunged free, the cuffs still on his forepaws, the chains tangling around his feet as he finally made it to a standing position. He shook himself hard, releasing the remains of the pain. And charged Frank's back.

Frank turned and tossed the ax at him. Dom dodged but not fast enough to avoid the sharp edge all together. The metal bit into his back hip, before hitting the wooden floor with a hard thunk.

The shock of pain only slowed him for a half a beat

before he leapt toward Frank. The wolf dodged away, thrusting out with the cattle prod. But this time he missed. Nick came up behind Frank before the wolf could move and wrapped his arms around the wolf's upper body, keeping his arms low and pinned. Frank stuck the prod into Nick's foot, and Nick howled, his hold on the wolf loosening.

Frank leapt away, facing both brothers from the opposite side of the cabin, his gaze focused on them, tracking their movements as they neared. Dom lowered into a crouch, readying to jump, but before he could, Frank raced toward the front door. Dom spun to cut him off, only to realize Jane was there, standing square in the middle of the only way out of the cabin.

And Frank was barreling right for her, so fast Dom couldn't get between them in time.

J ane felt the tiger's angry roar in her bones, but she didn't take her eyes off the blur of movement swarming toward her.

She couldn't really see the werewolf, he moved too fast, but she'd had a split second when she'd come through the door, a second when all three shifters were motionless and she could tell which blur was which.

She'd already had her gun raised and aimed when Frank charged her, which was just as well because she fired without thinking, an instinctive compression of the trigger that wasn't actually associated with conscious effort.

That reaction saved her. The shotgun jerked upward

slightly but she was used to the kickback, so her second shot was only a little off her first. The blur that was the approaching wolf froze, stopping so suddenly, she blinked at the solidness of him. He stared at her, then looked down at his chest, at the gushing, smoking hole that was the size of her fist.

She couldn't tell if she'd hit him with both cartridges, but at least one had been on target. At first, all she could see was the blood. She didn't hunt, though she'd learned how to handle a shotgun when she was a teenager. And since moving to Eirene, she'd practiced at the shooting range a lot with the shotgun because she refused to have a weapon in her house that she wasn't completely confident in using. She'd even ensured Ben knew how to handle the thing just in case. But she wasn't a hunter. She'd never actually shot another living thing. And watching the blood pour out of the wolf made her gag.

Then things got a lot weirder. The wolf howled, the cattle prod he still held dropped to the ground, and the smoke around his wound got stronger, like his insides were on fire. Jane gaped as the thug dropped to his knees, his chest heaving in and out, the movement too big for a human body to manage. She had the horrific thought that it was like watching a human-shaped balloon expanding past the popping point, except this balloon was smoking and burning and then...

His body exploded in a rain of blood and bones and putrid-smelling fire.

It happened so suddenly, despite the fact that she could see it coming, and she was too shocked to think about moving. A white blur materialized in front of her, rising up so high she couldn't see around it. For an odd moment, she thought it was an albino bear. But that wasn't right. In the next instant, she realized it was Dom, standing on his hind legs, blocking her from the gory explosion.

When he settled back onto all fours, she blinked past him at the bloody mess in the middle of the cabin. Then with a calmness that surprised her, she turned back out of the cabin door, went to the end of the porch railing, leaned over it, and threw up.

CHAPTER FOURTEEN

Jane swiped a hand over her mouth, then moved to the opposite side of the porch, where it didn't smell like her puke. She scooped up some fresh snow, pressed it into her mouth, let it melt, then spit it out. It helped wash the taste out somewhat, but her stomach still churned. She leaned heavily against the railing, breathing the cold air in deep, cleansing gulps. The fresh smells of the woods started to clear the stench of ruptured, burnt guts from her nostrils.

A moment later she felt a gentle hand on her back.

"Here," Dom said.

She glanced down where his arm had wrapped around her. He held a wrapped, red and white mint in the palm of his hand.

"Nick thought you might need this," he said.

She snorted. "Thanks." She leaned the shotgun—which she was surprised to realize she was still clutching—against the porch railing and pealed open the wrapper, popping the mint into her mouth. Its bright flavor helped settle her stomach as much as the fresh air.

"Can I ask you something?" Dom said, pulling her back into his arms, her back to his front.

She went willingly, wrapping her arms around his. "What?"

"Why the hell does my brother have mints in his pockets? He just scowled at me when I asked."

That made her laugh. "He got into the habit when Tiana had morning sickness. He'd grab handfuls from the bowl we keep next to the cash register to take home to her. Mints, actually most hard candies, can help with settling your stomach."

"I didn't know that. But Tiana gave birth five months ago. Why does he still have mints in his pockets?"

"Personally, I think he started eating them with Tiana and now he's addicted."

Dom chuckled and hugged her closer.

"Not happy at all about you hearing me throw up," she said after a minute. "Usually like to save that kind of thing for at least the fifth date."

"Are you okay now?"

"Yeah, yeah. I'm fine. Just need to…" She waved a hand in the air, not sure what she needed except for a little bit more fresh air. "I'll have to let Joe Sanchez know the silver buckshot works well."

Before Dom could respond, two men came charging out of the woods. Jane snatched up her gun and swung it to face the men, realizing too late that she needed to reload before the thing would be useful.

Dom reached around her and gently edged the shotgun muzzle down. "That's Gabriel and Adam Walsh."

"Ah. More werewolves." She kept her gun lowered but she didn't loosen her hold.

"Is everyone all right?" Adam said as the two men stepped onto the porch.

"Dandy," Jane said. "Except the bastard inside who is chum now."

Adam frowned past her at Dom.

"She shot Frank," he told the two newcomers. "Twice. Silver. It's…messy."

"Both cartridges hit him?" she asked. "Wasn't sure."

"One would have been enough," Dom said.

His arms around her waist tightened, a soothing support that she'd be embarrassed to admit she needed right then. Her knees were still trembling from the shock of having exploded a living thing.

The two newcomers went inside where Jane assumed Nick was waiting. She stayed on the porch, because there was no way in hell she'd be able to face the carnage in the cabin. Carnage she'd caused. Saving Dom.

That thought had her leaning back into him again, cradling his arms.

"I'm so glad you aren't hurt," she murmured. "You aren't are you?"

"Nothing that hasn't healed already."

"How about all that…stuff you stopped from hitting me

when that asshole…" She waved a hand vaguely in the air, not quite able to say it.

"Cleaned off when I shifted back to human," he said gently.

"Huh. Good to be a shifter."

He snorted a half-laugh. "I almost had a heart attack when I saw Frank start toward you."

"Seeing your blood outside your motel room took a few years off my life."

"You came to save me. My hero." He tightened his hold.

His comment made her blink, the thought settling in slowly—she'd been the hero this time. *She'd* come to save *him*. She'd been so intent on getting to him, ensuring Frank didn't hurt him, she hadn't really thought about *what* she was doing.

"Where's Ben?" he asked, distracting her.

"With the sheriff, fixing his email."

"Still in Eirene." He let out a long, relieved breath. "Good."

It made her heart tighten with all kinds of emotions— even though Dom had been the one in danger, he still thought about Ben's safety. She'd never been with anyone who was as concerned with her son's safety as she was herself.

Another realization that gave her pause. And something else to think about.

They stood there silently for a bit. The voices inside were quiet but intent. Sounded like some serious discussion going on, but she was too tired to eavesdrop. She'd ask

Dom about it later since she was positive he could hear every word.

Slowly, as her senses settled, a new realization sank in. She glanced down at Dom's arms—his bare arms.

She spun to face him. "You're naked!"

He grinned. "That happens when I shift and don't have any spare clothes to wear."

"It's freezing out. And you've been standing here naked for all this time!" She started to slip her coat off.

He stopped her. "Jane, you'll get too cold if you do that."

"I won't be naked. You're going to turn into an icicle if you don't cover up."

"I have a higher metabolism than you. I can take it."

She narrowed her eyes at him, hearing the slight hesitance in his voice.

He sighed. "If I stand still too long, yes, I will start to get too cold. But I'm okay for the moment."

"Will you be warmer as a tiger?"

"Of course. Fur coat and all."

"Then shift. I won't have you freezing to death after I've gone through all this trouble to save your sorry ass."

His lips twitched. "Fine. If it will make you feel better." He started to walk off the porch.

"Where are you going?" She reached for him to keep him from stepping barefoot into the snow.

"To shift. As ordered."

"Oh no you don't. Either here or inside, where you're not in the middle of the snow."

"I think you've seen enough tonight. You don't need to

watch me shift." He nodded toward the cabin. "There's a lot going on in there right now. I'll be fine in the snow. Trust me."

She frowned, about to argue over what she could and could not take, but he cupped her cheek, silencing her protest with the heat of his touch—warm palms despite the cold night air.

"I'll shift as fast as I can and be right back to you. Will you be…comfortable with me while I'm in my tiger form?"

"Yes." She shrugged. "Suspect I should start getting used to it. Seeing as how you're moving here and all."

He winced. "Beth Anne tell you?"

"Beth Anne knows?"

"She overheard me talking to Nick yesterday about houses in the area."

Jane chuckled. "I bet it's all she's been able to do not to spill that juicy bit of gossip. But Nick's the one who told me—I'm not sure he realized that's what he did at the time."

When Dom frowned, she glanced away. "I… When I hadn't heard from you all day, I called him to see if he'd seen you. And when he said he hadn't…" She was almost embarrassed to say this out loud, given what had actually happened to Dom. "I asked Nick if you'd left," she said quietly. "I thought… I was afraid you'd gotten what you wanted and left town."

"Damn it, Jane, if you don't know better than that by now, you have been deliberately ignoring what I've been saying this whole time."

He sounded both hurt and angry which made her feel even worse. But he also sounded sincere.

She sucked in a deep breath, metaphorically pulled up her big girl pants, and said, "I love you, Dom."

He stood stock still, blinking, his mouth hanging open, and the unadulterated shock in his expression made her grin.

He closed the small space between them, pulled her into his arms and kissed her, deep and hard, with a touch of desperation and a lot of emotion. She wrapped her arms around his neck and returned his kiss with everything she had in her.

She got lost in the relief and peace of Dom's kiss, savoring the heat of him, the taste of him mixing with the mint that had dissolved on her tongue. For a long moment, she forgot he was still naked. Until she felt his cock stirring against her hip.

She dragged her mouth from his. "Damn it, you distracted me. You need to go shift so you aren't cold."

"I am not even remotely cold right now," he said, trailing his lips down her throat. "In fact, I'm the very opposite of cold."

She shivered, not cold either. "Still…" She sounded breathy and unconvincing. That was embarrassing. Except with Dom, she didn't really care.

Before she could say more, the voices from inside got louder and the three men stepped out onto the porch.

Dom stopped kissing her but didn't loosen his hold when he turned to look at the werewolves. "We good here? I need to get Jane home."

Nick glanced at him then back at the Walsh brothers. "We're good. They'll take care of the clean-up."

"Least we can do," Adam said, scowling slightly.

"Damn straight," Jane said. "What about Eirene?"

The two wolves exchanged looks, and Nick smiled a little.

"They're going to make sure the pack knows the towns-folk all have silver bullets now," Nick said.

"A good supply of them," Jane added, not quite a warning—but almost.

"Our…more difficult wolves will stay away from town from now on," Gabriel said. "They're going to help with the clean-up here, just so they see what silver could do to them."

Jane glanced between the three men. "What about Siob-han's shop? She staying around?"

Gabriel looked to Nick.

Nick shrugged and said, "On probation. If there aren't any more problems, and we don't have to use any more silver bullets, then the shop stays."

"Good," Jane said. "She's got the cutest little baby outfit there I wanted to get for Chrissy for Christmas. Would hate to see the shop close before I got it."

Dom's lips twitched and he dropped a kiss on her head. Nick grinned, and somewhat to her surprise, so did Adam.

"If everything is settled then," she said, "I need to get home and check on my boy."

"We'll go get what we need to clean this up," Gabriel said, gesturing toward the cabin. To Nick, "I'll let you know when everything is taken care of."

Nick nodded. Then the two wolves disappeared into the trees, moving so fast Jane barely saw them leave.

"Jesus, you people are fast," she muttered.

"Speaking of which," Nick said. "You want me to carry you again, get you back to the truck. It'll be better if Dom shifts to his tiger in this weather."

"Again," Dom said, frowning down at her.

"He had to carry me here or it would have taken too long."

"So now both my brothers have had a chance to carry you?"

"I suppose so." She had to press her lips together so she didn't grin. "That bother you?"

"Hell yes. It's my turn." And without waiting for her to respond, he picked her up in his arms.

"Dom, you are still naked. You cannot run me through the woods like this."

"Watch me," he said.

And then they were running. So fast, she lost her breath. The speed blurred the trees and the slight queasiness of motion sickness rose, but as she held tight to Dom, she realized it wasn't as bad as it had been with Mitch and Nick. Being in Dom's arms was actually…nice. Fun. And as she snuggled closer to his heat and the yummy scent of him, she realized she could get used to this running at superfast speeds with Dom carrying her. She even let out a little laugh when he leapt over something, the move making her stomach drop like she was on a roller coaster ride.

By the time they reached the truck, she was grinning.

"You know what," she said into his ear. "I like that with you."

"Good. I'll be the only one carrying you from now on."

"It turns me on when you get all jealous and possessive, you know."

He growled, deep in his throat, and kissed her. She might have savored the kiss longer, but Nick cleared his throat, and she realized they weren't alone.

"I've got some spare clothes on the back seat," Nick said, opening the truck door so Dom could set Jane inside.

Nick slid her gun onto the floor under the seat, reminding Jane she'd forgotten all about it. That had been a dumb move. She blamed Dom's kiss for the distraction.

Dom dressed quickly then settled into the front seat next to her, holding her to his side as Nick drove them all back to Eirene—home.

CHAPTER FIFTEEN

J ane cradled her spiked hot chocolate and studied the crowd from the edge of the huge living room. Giant windows flooded the open, two-story space with late-afternoon light. A fireplace to one side crackled with a cozy fire. Bold blue rugs covered the polished wooden floors, and the furniture was all comfortable, huge, and mostly white—a very impractical color as far as Jane was concerned.

Several separate conversation areas filled in the giant open room—a large couch, coffee table and chairs to one side, a collection of five chairs around a small round table in another part of the room, a third collection of chairs and a small couch near the fireplace. Jane would have thought that kind of set-up would remind her of a hotel lobby, yet it didn't, instead making the room feel more intimate and comfortable. Strings of white holiday lights sparkled from a balcony railing overhead and covered every available space in the living room. Gold and silver holiday decorations and centerpieces with white candles and a combination of green and gold foliage adorned the various tables and the mantle above the fireplace.

Scattered around the room were silver platters covered with scrumptious hors d'oeuvres, provided by Nick and Lulu. And against the wall opposite the huge windows, a small bar was being manned by Tiana's brother Ethan, who was busy mixing some tasty concoctions for everyone—including Jane's hot chocolate laced with whiskey. Speakers set into the walls filled the area with quiet classical music that mixed with the laughter and chatter of the group. The house smelled of pine and delicious food.

Elizaveta had rented one of the largest cabins in the area—a multi-story architectural masterpiece that Jane had always wondered about. A corporation had built it just outside of Eirene about five years earlier, a year after Nick had moved to town, and the cabin had always seemed a pretty extravagant rental, given it was some distance from most of the ski resorts. Jane would have expected a place like this closer to Vail, but all the way out in Eirene…?

Looking at how comfortable Elizaveta was in the space, Jane was starting to suspect the older woman had built the cabin. Giving herself a place to stay and keep tabs on her grandson without being too obvious. Clever woman.

Jane grinned and sipped her rich drink, savoring the chocolate and whisky.

Dom joined her at the edge of the party and wrapped his arm around her waist.

She leaned into him. "So, how did you and Grace get along?"

"She said to tell you she approves."

Jane snorted. "I'll confirm that later."

She glanced around and saw her best friend emerging from the kitchen, making her way to the bar. Grace had arrived in Eirene that morning, and Elizaveta had insisted she join the family gathering. Dressed in a pair of black slacks and a dark blue silk shirt, with her white blond hair done up in an elegant French twist, Grace fit right in with the rest of the Chernikov clan.

Grace caught Jane's eye and winked, her grin huge as she nodded at Dom.

"Told you so," Dom said, sounding a little smug.

Jane just laughed. Grace approving of Dom was the icing on the cake of Jane's happiness, and any hint of hesitance she might have still had vanished—not that she'd have been able to change things anyway. She was well and truly in love with the man. But knowing Grace liked him was a nice bonus.

"My relatives haven't been pestering you while I've been making a good impression with Grace, have they?" he asked.

"Of course not. I love your family."

She gestured with her mug toward where Elizaveta sat on the huge couch next to Ben as Ben showed her something on his tablet. Elizaveta took the tablet from him, tried to do something, scowled and handed it back to him. Ben grinned, flicked a few things, then passed the tablet back to her.

"He's teaching her how to play some zombie game," Jane said. "She's taking it very seriously." She grinned when Elizaveta crowed in triumph and showed the tablet to Ben. Ben clapped.

"My grandmother is a very competitive person," Dom said. "But it's nice to see her getting along with Ben."

Jane heard something in his voice that made her look up at him. "You were worried about that? She's always been kind to him in the past."

"That was before you and I were involved."

He spoke quietly, but not so quietly she didn't hear him. "Why's that make things different?"

He sighed. "Tigers are…not always kind when it comes to differences." He paused, sipping the bottle of beer he held in one hand. Finally, he said, "You know my mother killed herself?"

"I do now."

"Nick's never told you about our past?"

"Not that much." She leaned into him. "You don't have to say more if you don't want to."

"No. This is something you need to know if you're going to be with me. Most tigers, aside from our family, don't have much time for the Chernikovs. My grandmother's powerful, but my brothers and I were marked by my mom's suicide and my father's…mental breakdown afterward. Because of the extinction issues, tigers take a very dim view of mental illnesses that might damage the already tight gene pool."

She let that sink in for a long time as she watched Ben and Elizaveta play. Tiana settled next to them, holding a squirming Chrissy. Elizaveta showed them the tablet, Ben said something, and everyone smiled—including the baby.

"So," Jane said, "in your world, Ben would be considered…what?"

"Damaged."

The stark word made her narrow her eyes as anger built. "My baby is not damaged."

"I know that. You know that. Other tigers…are less tolerant."

"Anyone says something 'less tolerant' about my boy to me, and I'm going to kick their asses."

"I know. I would, too. For the most part, we'll avoid the tiger world. There's no reason for you to have much to do with other tiger shifters outside my family. You or Ben, for that matter. But you should understand that prejudice is there in my world."

"You have it?"

"You know better than that."

"But you were worried about your grandmother?"

"Yes. Not because she doesn't love Ben as he is. But because I'm her grandson. And she hasn't been allowed to protect me from the other tigers—a deal she made to pay for her own son's life. He… In his grief, my father killed a human—a very bad man who was beating a woman, but the circumstances didn't change the consequences. Remember, killing a human is an automatic death sentence for a tiger shifter. Elizaveta paid a lot to ensure her youngest boy didn't suffer that fate."

Jane nodded, watching the older woman grin at baby Chrissy and chuck her under the chin to make her giggle.

"That must have been really hard on her," Jane murmured. "I'd have been desperate to save Ben's life, too."

Dom hugged her a little tighter. "Anyway, it's all history now. But my grandmother is as protective of us as she's allowed to be. I know she likes you."

"But you were worried she wouldn't want you shacking up with a human who had a damaged son."

"Don't ever say those words about Ben again," he growled.

And she grinned. "Your word, not mine, and I've heard that horrible shit before. You were right to worry about that because if Elizaveta, or anyone else for that matter, insults my son, I will not take kindly to it." She nodded at the group on the couch. "But I think we're okay. You haven't made any secret of our relationship since I arrived. She's too smart to miss it. And yet she's still playing with Ben." Jane turned in Dom's arms and looked up at him. "I suspect you underestimated your grandmother."

Dom kissed Jane gently. "Suspect you're right. Wouldn't be the first time."

She kissed him back, a quick brush of lips that set her nerves humming. Before she got caught up in it and embarrassed herself, she faced the crowd again. "So I know most everyone from the wedding. But who's the silver fox over there talking to Alexis?"

"Silver fox?" Dom growled.

Jane didn't try very hard to hide her smile. "Yeah, he is. Who is he?"

"He's too old for you," Dom said.

"Ha! That's funny when you consider I thought I was too old for you just a week ago."

"Right. Funny."

"I love when you get all growly and jealous. Makes a woman feel special."

"You are special to me."

Her heart jumped around in a giddy little dance. "You going to tell me about him or not?" she said, still not entirely sure how to deal with this joy suffusing her. "He looks like Grace's type," she added, not wanting to torture Dom too much.

"That's Alexis' uncle. The man who raised her after her parents were killed."

"He's looking annoyed. Can you hear what they're discussing with those super tiger ears of yours?"

Dom snorted. "I don't have to. Elizaveta has been nagging Xavier to join the elders' council."

She tried to remember what he'd told her about them. "They're your ruling body and you're missing one right now?"

"A space that needs to be filled but no one can agree on who should fill the position. It takes a lot of money and cunning and…well, you have to be a crafty sonofabitch."

"Like your grandmother?"

"Exactly," he said.

Jane laughed. "I take it sexy Uncle Xavier doesn't want to be an elder?"

"If you call him sexy again, I swear, Jane, I'm going to drag you to a private room and make you forget you've ever seen the man."

Her stomach tightened, her nerves tingled, and she purred a little, leaning into Dom. "You realize I might say it again just to get you to follow through with that promise?"

"I love you."

Grinning, she turned her face up for another kiss, this one a little more serious and a little less suitable for public. She eased away reluctantly. "You make me feel young," she said. "And giddy. And sexy. And all the things I haven't felt in forever. Thank you for that."

"You make me grateful," he said, very seriously.

She got lost in him for a moment, blinking when she realized they were making a scene—if anyone bothered to pay attention to them. Her cheeks heated and she faced the room again. To her amusement, Grace had insinuated herself into the conversation between Alexis and her uncle, and was making flirty eyes with sexy Uncle Xavier. Since Xavier looked pleased with Grace's flirting, Jane grinned.

"Told you he was Grace's type," she said. "So why doesn't he want to be an elder?"

"He's a very straight shooter, like Alexis. Not much tolerance or time for all the machinations of the council. He's rich enough and physically strong enough to be an elder. And better yet, he doesn't have a lot of enemies."

"But?" she asked.

"But the fact that he doesn't suffer fools lightly makes him a terrible diplomat. And some of an elder's job is more…diplomatic in nature."

"So he's not sneaky enough?"

"Exactly."

"Maybe that's exactly what your elders' council needs,"

she murmured, watching Grace casually touch Xavier's arm and Xavier stand a little taller.

Dom looked down at her, a funny little frown creasing the area between his eyebrows. "That's exactly what Elizaveta says."

"Huh." Jane looked back at the older woman still trying to work out the game Ben was teaching her. "Great minds, I guess," she said.

Dom laughed. "I think I'm in trouble."

"'Fraid so." She resisted saying more when Alexis' husband Victor joined her and Dom.

"Hey, Victor," Dom said aloud, signing the greeting at the same time.

Victor signed something back, then grinned at Jane, took her free hand and kissed her knuckles.

She felt her cheeks heating. "Hello, Victor," she said. Alexis' husband was the epitome of the tall, dark, and sexy, even with the few strands of gray feathering through his dark hair. "Are you having fun?" she asked.

He signed something that Dom translated as, "Having a great time."

When Victor signed something else at Dom, Dom said, "He's doing good so far. Caught up with the new technology really fast given he's more than eleven years behind the times. He'll make supervisor faster than anyone who's ever worked for me who started where he did." To Jane, Dom said, "One of Victor's oldest friends is working for me now. Don't discuss it with Mitch."

"Why not?"

"Long story. Let's just say Joseph got on Mitch's bad

side more than a year ago and Mitch isn't quick to forgive him."

Victor signed something, Dom signed back. Jane frowned at them.

Dom shrugged. "It has to do with Nila. Nila has forgiven Joseph. Mitch just holds grudges." Dom waved the topic away. "Anyway, it's history now. Joseph has become a really valuable employee since he started working for me a few months back."

Victor clapped Dom on the shoulder before forming the one sign in sign language Jane recognized—*thank you*. Then he pointed at Jane's now-empty mug and raised his brows.

"I'd love another," she said. "Thanks. Tell Ethan not to skimp on the whiskey."

Victor grinned big, took Dom's empty bottle, and went to the bar.

"So you gave Victor's friend a job even though it pissed Mitch off?" she asked when they were alone again.

"Mitch understands. He just doesn't want to talk about it."

Jane smiled and bumped against Dom so he would put his arm around her again. She leaned into him, sighing at the lovely family warmth in the room. And outside of her, Ben and Grace, every person in that room was a tiger shifter. Jane still couldn't quite believe this was her life, that beings she hadn't even known existed were now her... well, her family.

A family she loved.

Heart thumping a little harder, she tried to affect a

casual tone when she said, "So you know Mindy Jenkins, owns the antique shop?"

"Of course," Dom said, a question in his tone.

She kept her gaze on the room. "Seems her and her husband are selling his old cabin—had it in his bachelor days, kept it out of sentiment. Mindy's finally talked him into letting it go."

"Really."

Dom had gone very still next to her.

"Nice place," Jane said. "Plenty big enough. And it's relatively close to my house, just a short drive away. Since you were looking for a place here in town."

"I am. Would you… You think I should buy Mindy's cabin?"

"Well, your choice of course. It's nice." She paused, her heart thumping even harder as she said, "Of course, you could always move in with me."

For a long moment, she wasn't even sure if he was breathing. She waited until she couldn't stand waiting any longer, then she looked up at him from beneath her lashes. He was staring straight ahead, his expression completely unreadable.

The longer she stared, the harder her pulse pounded, the more worried she got. She'd pushed too hard, too fast. He wasn't ready for that yet. She opened her mouth to take back her offer, when he finally turned and looked down at her.

Her words clogged in her throat.

"You would really move in with me?" he asked, his voice quiet but urgent. "You're comfortable with that?"

"I asked, didn't I?"

"Is that all you're ready for?"

She frowned. "What the hell are you talking about, Dom?"

He swallowed visibly, his sign of nervousness making her frown deepen.

"Jane, I love you."

She smiled and raised her brows. "I love you, too."

"Will you marry me?"

Her mouth dropped open. "You want…to marry me?"

He nodded. "I always have."

"No one's ever asked me to marry them before."

"I'll understand if you're not ready yet, but—"

She put her fingers over his mouth, stopping him. "I'd love nothing more than to marry you, Dom Chernikov."

His smile bloomed so bright it was like looking into the sun. She was blinded by it and content to have that be her last sight. He pulled her into a tight embrace, kissing her too hard and too serious for public. She didn't really care about that, though. Joy raced through her, filling her, overflowing in waves of love like she'd never expected to feel. And a satisfaction settled into her bones, a rightness that had been missing all these years.

When he finally eased back from the kiss, she was breathing hard and wondering if they could sneak out of the room without being noticed.

Her hopes on that count were dashed in the next instant when Ben called out from the couch, "Hey Dom, did you ask my mom to marry you yet?"

Her cheeks warmed intolerably in her embarrassment.

She was too surprised to even scold Ben for asking such a personal question in public.

Dom grinned and without looking away from her said, "Yes, I did. And she said yes."

"Finally!" Elizaveta said loudly. "It's about damned time, Dimtry. I was starting to think I'd have to arrange your love life, too." From the corner of her eyes, Jane saw Elizaveta lean in close to Ben and say in a false whisper, "I have to do everything in this family."

The room erupted into applause and whistles. Jane shook her head, so far past embarrassed now, she just gave in to it.

Dom chuckled. "Welcome to the family."

She kissed him again, ignoring the whoops and catcalls. Too happy to care. For the first time in her life, she wasn't worried about anything at all.

She knew in her heart, she'd finally made a good choice.

Thank you for reading What A Tiger Wants! I hope you enjoyed seeing Dom and Jane get their happy ending. For an excerpt from book 9, Taming Her Tiger, keep reading.

TAMING HER TIGER

EXCERPT TIGER SHIFTERS 9

CHAPTER ONE

Amy Donovan hurried up the wooden stairs to the fifth floor of the Brooklyn art studio, out of breath and trying not to panic about being late. Damned weekend subways. She cleared the huge, rolling steel doors and stepped into the brightly lit, high-ceilinged loft, winter sun pouring in from the wall of windows opposite her. The gray sunlight was augmented by the overhead lights, reflecting off the scuffed pale wood floors and bright white walls.

She sighed in relief when she saw the open session hadn't started yet.

The familiar smells of the art studio—paint, solvent, charcoal, paper, and canvas—filled Amy with that sense of belonging, settling into her bones. The familiarity helped slow her racing, panicky heartbeat as she made her way across the room to a free space. Easels, chairs, and tables were already arranged in a rough semi-circle around a central model platform, the piles of pillows in the middle of the platform were draped in neutral, tan sheets. A dozen artists, the monitor, and the model coordinator all hovered around the room. A few people stood in small groups, chatting and drinking take-away cups of coffee and tea. Others were already at chairs or easels, setting out their materials or flicking through their sketch books.

She waved at acquaintances and other studio members as she wove past a section of seats to her easel. This was the final long-pose session of a four-week cycle, her last opportunity to have the figure model in front of her while she finished her oil painting.

Thoughts of said model scattered her focus and she nearly tripped over someone's bag. Apologizing, she hurried to her spot, pushing the momentary lapse aside. She was a professional; this was a professional setting. She refused to entertain the strong feelings and longings she'd experienced when Ethan Gupta had first taken the dais three weeks ago.

It hadn't exactly been a sexual reaction, though that was part of it. She'd done so many life drawing sessions over the years, she didn't really view the nude models that way —she saw lines, shadows, proportion, perspective, angles, and light contrasts. Or at least she had before Ethan.

But her reaction to him had been a lot more than just the sexual punch of seeing a man as beautifully masculine and perfect as Ethan was in real life. It was more stunned shock, a realization that she was staring at an actual muse. Her brain had exploded with images, colors, a longing to capture…something. *Him.*

She didn't believe in muses, exactly. Not in the mythical sense of the word. She knew a good figure model could inspire and energize her and her art. She'd had the experience on numerous occasions. But with Ethan, everything was different. More instant, more overwhelming, more…vivid.

That first time, she'd even sensed him before he'd come into the room, as if he projected an aura of creative inspiration she could feel along the length of her spine without having to look at him. The fact that she could sense him now, even though she couldn't see him, even though she knew the feeling was just a figment of her imagination, left her edgy and anxious.

After that first three-hour session, she found herself counting the days until the next one, and the one after that. Yet a part of her also dreaded each session, dreaded that sense of being overwhelmed and awed. The sense that her skills would never be good enough to capture the purity of the inspiration he offered.

Settling into the area she'd used for the last three sessions, she focused on putting out her supplies, collecting her canvas from one of the storage lockers provided to regular members, organizing her brushes, setting up her palette, studying her progress on her painting, determining where she needed to make adjustments and what she'd need to do to get the work done today…

One of her dearest friends, Reese Jordan, sat down next to her in a place already set up and ready for the session to start. Reese was a superbly talented sketch artist, oil painter, and sometimes sculptor. He was also the person who'd originally directed Amy to this studio and encouraged her to become a member. They'd known each other since Amy had come back to the art world two years earlier, and now she couldn't imagine her life without him. At forty-three, Reese tended to treat her like a little sister, and he'd become the big brother as well as the art mentor Amy had never had.

He kissed her cheek. "I thought you were going to miss the class."

"Subways," she growled, making him grin.

On her other side, Devine, artist, gallery manager, and another of Amy's good friends, settled into her station, rubbing Amy's arm by way of hello. Despite being in her mid-thirties, Devine was ageless, with flawless, smooth skin, hair that changed colors and cut frequently—that week it was a beautiful pale lavender shaped to imitate a 1950s flip—and blue eyes she accented with perfectly penciled black liner drawn to make her eyes look tilted and cat-like. She'd confided to Amy once that her ever-changing look was designed to appeal to her clients because they expected artists to be eccentric and "artsy." Devine ran a gallery in Soho that catered to art collectors of the rich-but-not-very-knowledgeable type. She could sell sand in the desert and ice in the arctic.

And for reasons Amy had never figured out, Devine

kept encouraging Amy to take her art more seriously, turn it into an actual career. Despite Amy's insistence that it wouldn't happen anytime soon. Her refusal to accept the possibility of art as a career had never deterred Devine from nagging her about it.

Before Amy could say more than hello, the shuffling, shifting sounds of people settling into their seats distracted her. She looked past Devine…in time to see Ethan step out of the bathroom at the rear of the studio, near the storage lockers and slop sinks. He'd changed out of his street clothes and into his simple dark blue robe, a color that did fantastic things to his wavy dark hair and eyes. He paused at the back of the room to chat with the coordinator and monitor, smiling and relaxed.

Amy caught herself staring, her gaze drawn to the perfect shape of his mouth, the solid line of his jaw, the way his hair curled around his ear. She blinked a few times, trying in vain to look away. She felt like such a fool, such a cliché, becoming obsessed with a model. But once he came into the room, she had trouble concentrating on anything else. To her embarrassment, he glanced up and caught her staring. His soft smile and nod of greeting only humiliated her more. She nodded back and turned to face her canvas, heat crawling along her skin and making her scalp prickle. He wasn't on the dais yet. He wasn't hers to study. He was a skilled human being who deserved her respect and admiration—not her obsessive ogling.

"He's magnetic, isn't he?" Reese leaned closer and said. "I can't stop watching him either."

His voice was quiet, but Amy still looked around to see who might overhear them.

"He's just so damned good at holding these long poses and still being…present, isn't he?" Devine said. "It's like watching performance art every time he hits the platform."

"I keep forgetting I'm supposed to draw and not just stare," Reese said, chuckling. "If I don't sell this piece, the world has no taste whatsoever."

Amy smiled at that. Reese's oil paintings and charcoal sketches were displayed in galleries across Manhattan and Brooklyn. He was one of the most gifted artists she'd ever encountered, and his work sold regularly even in the competitive New York market.

"The world doesn't have taste, darling," Devine said. "That's why I have a job."

Reese snorted. "And we're all very grateful for the job you do."

Devine nodded at Amy's unfinished painting. "That'll be worthy of sale, too, when you're done."

Amy stared at the canvas, at the way Ethan occupied the scene she'd built around him, the long, muscled lines of his body draped across the pillows like an ancient god. "Maybe," she said noncommittally. More than her resistance to considering art as a profession, the thought of parting with this particular painting actually caused something tight and painful to collect in her chest.

The final shuffling and noise of preparation settled and silence descended around the room as Ethan stepped up to the platform and dropped his robe.

Ethan settled onto the pillows, using the tape set down by the moderator after the last session to resume the exact position he'd held for the last month. The pose was comfortable, his upper body resting against the piled pillows, one knee bent and one arm resting on that knee. He could recline like this for the thirty-minute period without it hurting too much and without drifting off to sleep.

He concentrated on his own body, putting himself in exactly the same angles as the weeks before. Keeping his mind off the beautiful artist just to his right.

Amy Donovan.

She caused him more difficulty than he'd ever had during a life drawing class. Usually, he let his mind drift into a zone that embodied the pose, managing to remain present without focusing on any of the artists around him. But an *awareness* of Amy kept him on edge the entire time. He'd been hyper attuned to her for the last four weeks, and it was all he could do to keep his body from showing just how much he wanted her.

After seeing her, catching her scent at the first session, he'd very nearly backed out of this job. It wouldn't have done his reputation in the art world any good, but for the sake of self-preservation, he'd almost made the sacrifice. Only a keen sense of wanting to finish what he'd started kept him coming back. That and sheer, stubborn pride.

By the end of the first session, he'd managed to convince himself that his reaction was just because Amy bore a resemblance to a woman Ethan didn't want to remember. The thick dark hair, the blue eyes, the pale skin were superficially the same as Siya's. Amy's hair was curly where Siya's had been straight. Amy was a little taller and curvier than Siya. But the similarities in appearance were hard to ignore. And they made a great excuse for dismissing his reaction to Amy. Nothing he had to worry about. He'd be over that superficial attraction by the time he saw her again.

Unfortunately, when he'd shown up for the second session, he'd had to admit he wasn't just struck by Amy's beauty. She *drew* him the way a magnet pulled metal. He found himself overly focused on her, aware of where she was even when he couldn't see her, conscious of the subtle shifts in her scent—honeysuckle and art studio and woman. A combination that set his blood on fire.

He'd had a very similar reaction to Siya. And that was the real danger.

He hadn't had that kind of reaction to any other woman before or since—until Amy. It felt a little like obsession, impossible to control, overwhelming and consuming. Like being around Amy was as necessary as his next breath. He hated that feeling more than just about anything he'd ever experienced before. The same kind of preoccupation with Siya had almost gotten him killed. He could *not* do that again. He'd come to New York to escape the memory of Siya and what she'd done to him. He'd refused to have anything to do with the tiger shifter world, outside of his immediate family, after that.

Amy was human, which should have made her safe. But she called to his tiger so strongly it reminded him of being around a tigress. Which meant he should avoid Amy Donovan at all costs.

And yet, he couldn't bring himself to cancel the remaining two sessions. He was a professional, it was just once a week for a few hours, and for the most part, Amy seemed intent on avoiding him. He assured himself all of that would make it easier, and he wouldn't have to sacrifice his reputation just to avoid a human woman who didn't seem particularly interested in interacting with him anyway.

Unfortunately, his keen sense of smell picked up her attraction, the spice of desire in her scent, the way it enhanced the womanly musk that was part of her essence. He wanted to disregard that flavor, to pretend he didn't know she wanted him, too. She never showed any signs of acting on the chemistry and lust. He didn't have to act on those feelings either.

But his tiger saw her resistance to her own desire as a challenge—a challenge that was impossible to ignore. So hard he'd found himself walking past her during each break at the third session, making excuses to exchange small talk with her, to pass a comment on the progress of her painting. Despite his efforts to resist, he still pulled in her scent, holding his breath to keep the flavors on his tongue as long as possible, savoring the complexity. And more often than he cared to admit, his mind wandered to more erotic thoughts, musings that had been invading his dreams during the intervening week. What her skin might taste like, feel like, what she'd look like stripped out of the loose jeans and t-shirt she always wore to the studio, what she'd look like in the throes of orgasm...

Those thoughts during a nude session were *not* good.

The entire room would notice his erection, which wasn't exactly the look he was going for with this pose. It happened to male models sometimes, and artists generally ignored it. But as a tiger shifter, Ethan rarely noticed being nude and never had trouble controlling his body while he was. He'd spent his life taking his clothes off in front of other shifters so he could let his tiger out. Unlike most humans, Ethan was as comfortable without clothes as he was with them.

Except with Amy Donovan in the room.

Even now, during what was thankfully the last session of the four-week cycle, it took a concerted effort on his part not to let his awareness of Amy show. The room was mostly silent except for the sounds of brushes lapping over canvas and pencils scraping across paper, or the occasional groan of a seat as someone adjusted their position. His pose kept his focus on a point in the room where the steel frame around one window butted up against the white wall, so he only caught glimpses of Amy from the corner of his eye. If he didn't focus on it, her scent blended in with all the other smells in the large, open space, just one more part of the complex essence of an art studio.

But even without trying, he still ended up parsing her scent out from the more complicated background. And her lust was there, tamped down by her concentration but still there, heady and rich…and tempting.

If it wasn't so quiet in the room, he might have groaned out loud.

This was the last session, he reminded himself. After this, he wouldn't see her again, and he'd go back to living his life without this preoccupation. He couldn't afford to lose his heart and soul to a woman again. In fact, he wasn't sure how much he had left to lose after the damage Siya had done. Amy called to that part of him, and he just couldn't give in to the desire and risk any more pain. So lust or no lust, Amy Donovan was off limits.

At the first break, he donned his robe and made a circuit of the room, stretching and loosening muscles that had gotten stiff over the last half hour. Some of the artists stopped him to make small talk. One or two gave him their cards, offering the possibility of future work. He managed to keep his distance from Amy, but only barely. His tiger kept urging him to walk past her, test her reaction to him, see if he could make her desire overcome her focus on her painting…

His focus on keeping Amy at a distance while still being utterly aware of her was his excuse for missing the feel of another tiger shifter nearby.

He frowned and glanced at the huge windows. What the hell was another tiger doing in this area?

Settling back onto the dais, Ethan opened his senses to that other shifter, trying to get a sense of who it was.

There were two other males in the city. When Ethan had moved here, they'd met to set up territorial boundaries which would allow them to remain neighbors without conflict. Of necessity, they did occasionally have to move through each other's territories, but those incursions were overlooked if they didn't last long or happen too frequently. Ethan specifically chose modelling jobs that avoided the other males' territories—usually in places that were neutral.

His freelance work as a tax accountant rarely brought him into contact with the others either.

He'd never sensed one of the other New York males nearby during his previous sessions here, but he supposed it wasn't out of the question for one to have come into Brooklyn for personal reasons. This was neutral ground, so there was no reason for one of the other males to avoid the area. And being New York, tiger shifters from other places did make their way into and through the city on business, travel, or just as tourists. But this area of Brooklyn wasn't on the typical tourist routes, and it was a Sunday afternoon, so there shouldn't be a lot of reason for a tiger to be here for business.

Despite his senses being fully open, the other shifter remained just at the edges of his awareness, too far to give Ethan much information. He couldn't even be sure if the tiger was male or female. He kept his attention on the shifter throughout the next half-hour period, and the tiger remained in the same place the entire time—maybe eating at a local restaurant?

When the break was called, Ethan blinked in surprise. He hadn't even noticed his wrist on his bent knee falling asleep. He rose, slipped into his robe, and wandered close to the big windows in his circuit to stretch his muscles. Glancing outside in hopes of catching sight of the other tiger didn't help. Whoever it was, they weren't in plain sight from the studio.

With his mind on the mysterious shifter, Ethan didn't realize he'd wandered close to Amy until her scent hit him hard. He fought off a scowl when he noticed he'd stopped just behind her. She didn't glance back at him, but she did sit a little straighter on her chair.

Cursing his unconscious pull to her, he made an effort to look at her painting so he could pass a comment as an excuse for why he was just standing there.

For a long moment, he stared at the painting, unable to actually form a coherent word. When he could speak, he said, very quietly, "That's magnificent. You're amazing."

Pleasure and surprise filled her honeysuckle scent with citrus and a touch of vanilla. He edged closer, unable to resist her, wishing there weren't so many people in the room watching this exchange.

Wishing he could back away before he lost his mind completely.

"Thank you," she murmured. She glanced over her shoulder, smiling shyly at him, her blue eyes sparking with pleasure through the fringe of her long lashes.

The sexy look combined with the husky sound of her voice hit him hard, right in the gut and lower. His blood pounded, his breathing sped. In that moment, he was extremely glad to have his robe on because his body reacted instantly. He took a half step closer to her when she faced her painting again, raising a hand to test the texture of her hair before he realized what he was doing. He snatched his hand back and with a grunt, he spun away from her and stalked to the farthest end of the studio.

Damn but she was dangerous. Without even trying. Even the puzzle of a strange tiger in the area couldn't fully distract him.

If he wasn't careful, he was going to give in to this lust, and to hell with the consequences.

He sighed when his tiger growled in his head—in approval.

**Look for Taming Her Tiger
Book 9 in the Tiger Shifters series
Out now!**

BOOKS BY KAT SIMONS

TIGER SHIFTERS SERIES

1 - Once Upon a Tiger

2 - Along Came a Tiger

3 - Here There Be Tigers

4 - Her Tiger To Take

5 - To Tempt a Tiger

6 - Down Will Come Tiger

7 - To Catch a Tiger

8 - What a Tiger Wants

9 - Taming Her Tiger

Tiger Shifters Series Vol 1 (Books 1 - 3)

Tiger Shifters Series Vol 2 (Books 4 - 6)

ABOUT THE AUTHOR

Kat Simons earned her Ph.D in animal behavior, working with animals as diverse as dolphins and deer. She brought her experience and knowledge of biology to her paranormal romance fiction, where she delights in taking nature and turning it on its ear. After traveling the world, she now lives in New York City with her family. Kat is a stay-at-home mom and a full time writer.

For more on Kat and her future books:

Website: http://www.katsimons.com
Newsletter: http://eepurl.com/OxQQL

www.ingramcontent.com/pod-product-compliance
Lightning Source LLC
Chambersburg PA
CBHW050510190726
48284CB00003B/765